THE BED HEADS

LIFE'S A TRIP

Cody Ashbury

WRITER'S WORKSHOP LLC

CASPER, WYOMING

Cody Ashbury @ Writer's Workshop LLC
301 Thelma Drive #226
Casper, Wyoming 82604
www.codyashbury.com

Publisher's Note: This is a work of fiction. Names, characters, places, and situations are a product of the author's imagination.   Any likeness to actual people, living or dead is purely incidental. Locales and public names are sometimes used for atmospheric purposes. Although they are real entities, the businesses, names, companies, events, institutions, or places referenced in this book do not imply their endorsement or interest in the characters, themes, or the book in general.

Characters, concept, and illustrations by Brandon Wardell
Design and editing by Jennifer Flaig

Library of Congress Control Number: 2018958500

ISBN 978-1-949605-02-0 (hardcover)
ISBN 978-1-949605-00-6 (paperback)
ISBN 978-1-949605-01-3 (ebook)

First Edition

This book is dedicated to the Grateful Dead,
whose philosophy, music, and legacy inspire
the creation of something new, every day.

Additionally, this is a tribute to all Dead Heads,
whether they've been on this grateful journey from
the beginning or are just now discovering the Dead.

Wishing you peace and love.

CONTENTS

LIFE'S A TRIP

The Bed Heads: Book One

PREFACE

Spoiler alert: This isn't really a spoiler, but it is important. Reading is more enjoyable when accompanied by music. It's true. Reading and music pair like eggs and ham. Like peanut butter and jelly. (Please don't pair those if you have a food allergy.) Like ice cream and summer. No, no... more like your perfect sweater on a chilly night while sitting around a campfire at your favorite place, by your favorite place, i.e. lakeshore, mountain top, curbside, etc. Trust us; we've thoroughly field-tested and researched all of this. For you.

Reading will make you smarter. In fact, reading this book while listening to our suggested playlists will make you the smartest. All right, by definition, not everyone can be the smartest. That's okay though, because we love you for who you are and who you will become. So achieve your greatest! Be smarter. Or smartest. Or somewhere in between, like smarterer. You might ask, "Did we invent that word?" It's entirely possible. But you're smart and we know you get what we're saying.

Books and music! That's a fact, Jack. For your convenience, we sprinkled song titles throughout this book. We've created online mixtapes of the soundtrack for the movie in your head. You can find curated playlists at thebedheads.org. Even better? Here's the direct link: https://wriwksp.com/groovytunes Test drive some tunes. Your eyes and ears will thank you. Most of all, your friends and loved ones (including your pets and probably your neighbor's pets) will thank you for the intellectual stimulation you bring to the relationship. We guarantee it.

(Disclaimer on guarantee: We made that up. Because we're writers. Of fiction. But if it makes you feel better, feel free to pay $39.95 for return shipping and handling, a 35% restocking fee, a 3.5% emotional damage tax, and the price of one group therapy session for our mothers who are always hopeful for our success.)

PRE-PROLOGUE

"Unknown Legend"
— *Neil Young*

PROLOGUE

"Simple Twist of Fate"
— Bob Dylan

Stanley scrolled through the camera roll on his phone, absentmindedly sipping a Peanut Butter Mocha blended beverage. His mouth was so cold he couldn't taste the peanut butter. He came across several images from the alumni center's exhibit about Casper College in the 1960s. Shiny new trucks and muscle cars in the parking lot. Vehicles that would be considered classics now. Brick buildings. A bowling tournament? Feeling the onset of brain freeze, he pressed his tongue to the roof of his mouth and set his ice-cold mocha on the table. Ignoring the sensation, he returned to focusing on the photos. One in particular caught his eye.

It was the picture of the main display case that had a video screen showing interviews from faculty and students of that era. He felt a familiar pull. His curiosity heightened, there was something special about one interview. Something he had meant to research. He retrieved a worn, leather book from his satchel and untied the cord. He began flipping through the pages until he found the note he'd written about a band. There it was. The Bed Heads.

He remembered watching a video interview of retired professor, Rubin Hart. Professor Hart had described The Bed Heads as a band started by five faculty members at the college. He'd talked about their plans to play at music festivals across Wyoming. After a series of frustrating disappointments, the band gave up on their dream. Stanley added a color-coded sticky flag to the page to remind himself to find out more. Their unfulfilled dream intrigued him. He knew what it was like when unforeseen circumstances steal a dream.

Thankful for Blue Ridge Coffee's Wi-Fi, he googled "The Bed Heads" on his laptop and found an old article by Oil City News. He quickly discovered that The Bed Heads had started in Casper and played local venues. There was Super 8 footage on YouTube of one of their performances. He found himself captivated by the band's music and their story.

He subscribed to the channel and watched the videos several times, pausing and rewinding, noticing something different with each replay. The audio wasn't high quality, but he could see their energy. He messaged the person who posted the video to see if he could find someone who knew more about The Bed Heads.

He moved to the window, the rolling mountains dwarfed by endless blue skies. He wasn't sure, but he thought he might be looking at Casper Mountain's ski slopes. He'd stumbled upon Hogadon Basin while exploring the mountain to find Beartrap County Park. It had been summer and he'd only walked around, checking out trail names, wildflowers, and ski lifts. About the only slope he'd be willing to try was "Morning Dew," which was for beginners. He heard his laptop chime with the notification of a new message. He read the reply from Jon Hart, who had uploaded the video about his father's band. He asked to meet with him and his dad. Jon replied that his father still worked part-time on campus.

Stanley returned to the internet to research the campus of Casper College. He'd been to the alumni center, but hadn't been to the college often enough to know his way around. He found a detailed map on their website. The maintenance building was located near the Tate Geological Museum. He opened Google Maps and planned his route using street view. As soon as he saw the life-sized dinosaur, he knew that building would be easy to find.

The next morning, he tracked down the T-Rex and quickly found the maintenance building. Stanley walked into the large shop area and saw a man in his early to mid-seventies standing next to a workbench. Stanley noticed that the man was fit, tan, and did not resemble someone who was likely almost seventy-five years old. He had a huge smile and hummed as his hands moved effortlessly to repair the commercial grade light fixtures that lay on the workbench. His body had a rhythm to it. His movements were like a graceful dance, with music flowing through every aspect of his being. This had to be Professor Hart.

"Professor Hart?" Stanley said, his voice full of hopeful expectation.

"The one and only, my man. Are you the guy my son told me about?"

"Yes, sir. I'd like to talk about The Bed Heads."

"One of my favorite subjects!" Professor Hart gestured towards a nearby stool. "Please, make yourself comfortable. If you don't mind, I'll keep working while we talk. Or better yet, I'll make us some coffee."

The maker hissed and gurgled while the shop filled with the comforting smell of freshly brewed coffee. Stanley looked around at the faded photographs pinned to the board by Professor Hart's desk. A motorcycle. Two boys wearing roller skates at what appeared to be a birthday party. A group of friends standing outside of a building downtown. Professor Hart interrupted his thoughts, handing him a cup of steaming brew. "It's been some time since anyone's shown interest in our music. It still plays in my head every day. For me, the music never stopped."

They spent the next hour talking about The Bed Heads. Professor Hart described the band and their jam sessions. "We weren't kids playing in a garage, isn't that what they call it nowadays? Garage bands? It sure felt free like that. Just enjoying the moment."

"Those videos of the band captured something special."

"My sons surprised me when they posted our videos to YouTube. They're thoughtful like that. They found a box full of memories a few years back, and started playing our old jam session reel-to-reel tapes. It was a real trip, man. Seeing my boys getting into our music."

Stanley leaned forward in his chair. "You have recordings of your jam sessions?"

"Yeah, my boys even converted the tapes to digital recordings. They gave me CDs for my birthday that year." Professor Hart paused, watching Stanley, his thoughts almost visible on his face. His eyes twinkled. "You seem genuinely interested. How would you like to borrow the CDs?"

"Hell yeah!" Stanley's voice echoed in the shop. He hadn't meant to show that much enthusiasm, but the offer caught him by surprise.

Stanley drove back to his apartment, cursing his old Wagoneer for not having a CD player. He parked in the first available spot and hurried inside. He loaded one of the CDs into the player, hit play, and upped the volume.

Sitting in his bean bag chair, he closed his eyes and listened. The music was raw, passionate, and real but something was missing. Like it wasn't finished. The band hadn't reached their full potential. They sounded close to the original artists they were covering. Every so often, there'd be a moment that felt different. A note held longer. A slight variation on a riff. But then it'd stop, as if they self-corrected, abandoning their improvisation in favor of the recorded version of the song. He wondered how the band's sound would have developed over time if given the chance. If they had kept improvising and experimenting with different ways to play.

A few days later, he returned the CDs to Professor Hart who was once again in the maintenance shop on campus. He smelled coffee as soon as he opened the door.

"I had a feeling you'd be back today," Professor Hart said. "You're just in time for coffee."

Stanley couldn't help but smile. He liked this guy. "Being predictable isn't as bad as people make it sound. Not if it gets you coffee. Thank you for sharing those recordings with me. I love the band's sound."

"Yeah, man," Professor Hart said, pouring coffee into two ancient looking mugs. "We were just a group of faculty who loved music and loved jamming."

The coffee was strong. And tasty. "Do you have any recordings of your live stuff? Not from jamming, but at a gig? I can only imagine how awesome you sounded at a venue. In front of an audience. The YouTube audio wasn't very clear."

"Yeah, we had a good time. Crowds dug us. We didn't record those shows. We wanted to. We had this dream of touring and recording. But it never really happened."

"That's a shame. What went wrong?"

"Well, let's just say we lacked reliable transportation. We fixed up this totally psychedelic bus. We loved that thing, but it was hard to get to gigs when you spent more time fixing it instead of driving it. So, we stopped trying to tour and just jammed at Wavey Davey's place in Alcova. Last time I saw that bus, it was in a junkyard off Poison Spider Road."

Stanley set his coffee on the workbench and picked up a crescent wrench. He threaded the center adjustment until the jaw opened to its fullest extent. Then he threaded it back the other way. And open again. He hesitated, knowing he needed to ask Professor Hart the question going through his mind. He had to work up the courage. This was too important to mess up. Stalling, he engaged in small talk, continuously opening and closing the wrench's jaw. Finally, with a blast of courage he sputtered, "Don't you wish you could go back in time? And change things?"

Professor Hart, sensing his uneasiness, chuckled and replied, "Sometimes I wonder what life would be like if we did go further. It'd be a trip, that's for sure."

Stanley put the wrench on the bench and reached into his satchel to grab his journal and a pen. Choosing his words carefully, he said, "When was the moment you realized the dream was over?"

Professor Hart thought for a minute. "Well, I guess it was the first time we took the bus out. It broke down just north of Kaycee and we didn't make it to the festival. We had it towed back to Wavey Davey's house and got it going again. Then after two more breakdowns and missed shows, we couldn't get festival gigs. The dream was over."

"That must have been disappointing. I'd love to see The Bed Heads make it. I'll bet it'd be amazing," he said, writing in his journal.

"Yeah, that would have been incredible."

Stanley thanked him again and left campus to go to Blue Ridge Coffee. He needed a Health Muffin and some dark roast. He paused in the parking lot to take a long look at the mountain and breathe in the crisp, clean Wyoming air. He made a mental note to attend the next Beartrap Summer Festival.

As he sat near the fireplace, he tapped his fingers on the table in contemplation. "A bus?" he said to himself. "I can't believe their dream ended just because of a broken-down bus." He took a drink of his coffee, its bitterness balancing the sweetness of the muffin. He wondered how different it would be now if The Bed Heads had been able to fix their bus when it had broken down the first time. They could have toured throughout Wyoming to play at festivals. He imagined how much their sound would have matured and evolved. The jam session tapes and the old video footage impressed him. He could see their future playing in his head like scenes from a movie.

He spent several minutes thinking about the consequences of interfering with the space-time continuum. He'd been lucky this far. He'd need to be careful if he did it again. He picked up his phone and found the picture from the alumni exhibit. He opened his journal to the note about what Professor Hart had said. He wondered how much the exhibit would change if The Bed Heads fulfilled their dream. All it would take is to manipulate one variable. Fixing the bus could change everything for The Bed Heads. He could build a time bridge to the exhibit. He'd have to research the band and its members to determine exactly how and when to help. He'd need to find the precise moment to anchor the time bridge. It was a balancing act. He could influence the situation, but they'd ultimately be responsible for their future.

Looking at his phone again, he willed the alumni exhibit to tell him what to do. Should he give them a second chance? He decided it was worth the risk. After all, it's more than just ashes when your dreams come true.

ORANGE TUPPERWARE

"Attics of My Life"
— Grateful Dead

Davey sat on the back porch sipping his morning coffee as he watched antelope graze in the yard. He wondered when his friend, Bear, would return. It had been several weeks since he had seen him, but it was not unusual for Bear to be gone for periods of time and then suddenly come around again. He had been alone for most of the summer break. The loneliness was wearing on him.

He turned his thoughts to the upcoming fall semester. It wasn't the academics or structured schedule he was looking forward to, even though he enjoyed having a routine and a defined purpose. He looked forward to being around and engaging with the faculty and students who would converge on the campus in the next few weeks. He just didn't want to be alone any more.

Summer break had been warm and pleasant providing Davey the opportunity to enjoy his rural sanctuary. Every day, he would travel the half a mile up his lane to the highway to get his mail. As he rambled along the lane, he enjoyed the wildflowers that had bloomed along either side and looked for wildlife with which he shared the property. In the afternoon, he would walk the trail leading down the butte to the lake. He spent time by the lake listening to the ripples sing to him as they rolled onto the sandy shore. He enjoyed the songs of the birds and the rhythm of the wind. It was like all of nature was performing a concert to soothe his weary soul. It did for that moment, but soon the uneasiness would return. He thought of his wife and children. He knew he had a promise to keep and a decision to make.

To him, time traveled at a different pace, speeding up some days and slowing down others. It seemed like only a few weeks had gone by, when in reality, it had almost been a year since his wife of 35 years had passed. The cancer had spread quickly throughout her body. She passed away only six short weeks after her diagnosis. The sudden loss of his best friend left him stranded on an emotional roller coaster. He felt the warmth of the morning sun as it made its way over the eastern mountains to cast its brilliance on the far buttes, causing the lake to shimmer.

He thought about the day he and his wife had driven from Casper to Alcova Lake to look at the house. As soon as she saw the view, his wife decided they should purchase it. They hadn't even toured the house yet. They bought a forty-acre farm that had a house, barn, and outbuildings. The property sat a half a mile south of Highway 220 on the heights overlooking the lake. Positioned on the back third of the property, the house was perfectly placed to see the lake and the surrounding views of the red butte to the south, the open prairies to the north, and foothills on the east and west. The lane off the highway ran by the house and curved around to the barn and outbuildings. Their farm was a wonderful place for their four daughters to transition from childhood to adulthood. He thought about how their youngest was now in her mid-twenties. He wondered what his daughters were doing today and when they'd be able to visit again.

This summer had been abnormally quiet. He was used to a summer filled with traveling, music festivals, and nature. He had miles of memories with his wife and family, traveling around the state, having adventures, and enjoying all the little moments, the ones you'll miss if you're not paying attention. He knew he needed to bring "the music" back. His wife had said something during the last few days of her life that stuck with Davey. She said, "Remember, make sure the music never stops. Promise me. After I'm gone, you will never let the music of life, joy, and adventure stop for you."

Over the past year and especially this past summer, he had found it difficult to keep his promise. Not that he hadn't tried. He made plans to attend his favorite music festival, even intending to stay two extra nights near Cheyenne. But it hadn't felt the same to go on a road trip by himself. He didn't have anyone to help him spot bald eagles along highway 25 near Wheatland or to share an acknowledging smile when a band played a familiar song. His heart just wasn't in it, so he had left the festival early and driven home.

He took another swallow of his coffee. The unexpected coldness made him aware that he had been sitting there for a while. He chuckled to himself as he realized he had been so lost in his thoughts that the time had passed without his noticing. He stood up, stretched, and walked through the back door into the kitchen. He paused, looking at the turquoise refrigerator and stove. He couldn't help but smile as he remembered all the discussions he'd had with his wife as they made their color choice. His wife had wanted a bright and cheerful kitchen.

It had delighted her when Davey found a white laminate counter top speckled with yellow, pink, and turquoise. She quickly found yellow fabric with pink, turquoise, and orange flowers to make curtains that would hang in all ten windows in their kitchen and breakfast nook. She had finished her decorating by covering the seat cushions of the chairs and benches for their maple table. With a smile of remembrance, he sighed and rinsed out his coffee mug.

He headed out of the kitchen, turning right to walk down the chartreuse hallway to the dining room. They had only used this room for formal occasions, like when they had company over to fondue and, after the girls left, for family get-togethers. Over the past few years, he and his wife ate dinner in the kitchen. They would eat breakfast and lunch on the back porch when the weather permitted and sometimes even when it did not. They enjoyed the view from the breakfast nook that looked over the back five acres of their land, across the lake, and to the red buttes to the south. He ran his hands along the blue and green floral wallpaper that lined the walls of the dining room. He grinned as he remembered how his two oldest daughters would sit at the table, running their fingers across the raised textures of the lines.

He walked through the dining room and into the parlor. He stood in the parlor doorway, looking at the piano that hadn't been played in a long time. He realized that he hadn't listened to a single 8-track or record since his wife had passed. Just before her diagnosis, he bought her a General Electric Scandia stereo console with a flat walnut veneer. She hadn't seen cassettes before and he thought she might like to record a song on the piano for the girls, but they never had a chance to do so. His eyes swept the room, taking in its cherry-red area rug surrounded on three sides by a blue paisley chair, an orange crushed velvet sofa, and two gold swivel chairs. Time was frozen on the cuckoo clock since he hadn't wound it in months. His wife had wanted the room to feel open and ready for music and dancing.

He walked back through the dining room and into the hallway. He continued down the hall to where it opened into the foyer. The library was on his right, the staircase leading to the second floor was on his left, and the front door was straight ahead. He turned to look at the framed pictures lining the stairs. Most were of his daughters, but there were a few of his whole family. And even one of the sweet dog they had when the girls were little.

He looked around the foyer and noticed for the first time that there were still Tupperware containers on the telephone table from the food people had brought over after his wife's funeral. He'd washed and stacked the containers near the door with the intention of delivering them, but never had. Now he noticed the variety of earthy colors in the Tupperware and thought about how his wife preferred orange. She liked the way the orange canisters looked near her turquoise stove. He gathered the containers in his arms and walked into the library. His girls had loved how the first floor of the house was like a square donut, as his oldest daughter had pointed out. They'd run laps around the center staircase, racing through the hallways.

He spent most of his time in the library. With its olive-green shag carpet, orange chairs, oak typewriter desk, wood paneling, and filled bookshelves, he found the room comforting.

The stone fireplace matched the exterior of the house. He moved to the desk and picked up his tin from Donells Candies, sat down in his favorite green recliner, and thought about how he hadn't walked around the other half of this floor in several months. He wasn't sure how long it had been since he'd gone upstairs. The last time had probably been when Bear helped him put the folding chairs back in the storage room. The girls had gone home and Bear had stopped by to see how he was doing. After the last trip up the stairs, they'd walked around for a few minutes, looking at the views through the windows. Bear had even joked about how much space there was and how the bedrooms were like little apartments he could rent to colleagues.

Without his wife, his home had slowly become just a place to live. It seemed like yesterday that the girls were drawing on the walls and playing in the yard. He could not remember when someone had occupied the rooms for any length of time or gathered in the kitchen for Sunday morning breakfast. Could he and his girls be that old? He remembered when the house was filled with music, laughter, and joy. All that remained were the echoes and layers of sweet memories.

After the girls moved out, they would come back and visit for long weekends, holidays, birthdays, and even the summer festival on Casper Mountain. His wife was good at planning family get-togethers. He enjoyed the reunions that brought smiling faces of spouses and grandchildren back to visit. Since his wife had passed, he noticed a great void in his home, in his heart, and in his life. It wasn't necessarily sadness, but more of an awareness that the music had faded. He knew it was time to bring the music back to his life.

As he sat in his favorite chair, he opened his tin of chocolates and popped a Dark Chocolate Pecan Cluster in his mouth. He chewed slowly and made a plan. First on his list was to deliver that Tupperware.

2

GROOVY APPLICANTS

"I Need a Miracle"
— Grateful Dead

The next day, Davey woke up early. "It's time," he thought to himself as he sat in his office on campus to draft an advertisement to post on the faculty community bulletin board. He wrote some thoughts for the wording and realized that he wasn't well versed in the current vernacular. He would ask Bear, but he hadn't called back yet. Instead, he phoned his youngest daughter for a consult. She suggested describing the rooms as groovy, outta sight, fab, or neato. He finished the ad and walked down the hall to the bulletin board. Before he could change his mind, he grabbed a push pin and secured the ad to the board. The ad read as follows,

"For Rent...

Established country home with four groovy rooms.

Transportation to the College available.

If interested, please call Davey at 555-867-5309."

"Well, it's done," he thought to himself. Turning away, he wondered if this was the right decision. He would bring strangers into his home. They would create memories that did not include his wife and the girls. He hesitated and wondered if everyone would get along. He walked into the bathroom to give himself a pep talk in front of the mirror. His second youngest daughter, now a counselor, told him to try this technique anytime he struggled with a decision. He'd felt silly at first, but she'd assured him it would work. He looked at his reflection, squared his shoulders, smiled and said, "You're doing the right thing. You're inviting the music back. You're making new friends and memories. This is the right path."

With confidence in his decision, he returned to his office and stared at the phone.

As he waited, he wondered if he would he get any responses to his advertisement. He worried that his colleagues wouldn't realize he had posted the ad since he hadn't used his nickname on the sign. His friends and family call him, "Wavey Davey," because he was always smiling and waving at friends and strangers alike. No matter how it turned out, he knew he was ready for this next step and whatever adventure it brought to his life. He would be open to it.

Within an hour, the phone rang. He was pleasantly surprised at the quick response. He received several more inquiries that day from non-tenured faculty who were exploring options before renewing their one-year leases and tenured faculty looking for long-term lease opportunities. The semester would start soon and the demand for housing was high.

Over the next few days, he answered calls, took names of the people interested in a room, and gave tours of the house. He brought the applications home so he could sit at the kitchen table, drink coffee, and choose his future tenants. He knew he could exclude the folks who did not want to commute to the college or did not like rural living. That left him with nine applicants. He spread the nine applications out on the table to get a bird's-eye view. His gaze fell on the hygiene question, and he pulled out the two applications where they had circled "No" indicating it was not important to them. He looked at the responses for hobbies and pastimes. Although he was intrigued, he removed the application for "riding my chopper up and down your carpeted halls," thinking that this could be dangerous to the other tenants. And to his carpet.

The first tenant he chose was Joey, a tenured professor from the School of Fine Arts and Humanities. Joey was about 15 years younger than Davey but could have easily been mistaken as a contemporary. He had seen Joey around campus and had been on committees with him over the past few years. Joey had a great countenance about him that shone through his burly yet refined exterior. He thought that Joey was warm and witty and had always appreciated the fact that Joey never took anything too seriously.

During the tour of the house, Joey picked up a piece of scrap metal by the shed and offered to make a new mailbox. He hadn't made one before, but said he'd figure it out. Joey was always looking for new experiences and adventures. As an artist, he found celery Jell-O an excellent base for savory concoctions. Square carrots, round peas, bits of potato, and oval hard-boiled eggs, all suspended in gelatin. Joey's enthusiasm for Jell-O salad reminded him of the time his wife participated in National Use-Up-Your-Leftovers-in-a-Jell-O-Salad week. It had been an interesting seven days.

The next tenant he chose was Stella. She was starting her fifth year at the college teaching chemistry, biology, and physical sciences. He knew most, if not all, of the faculty at Casper College. He had only seen Stella at a couple of mandatory faculty wide meetings. He asked a few of his colleagues about her. They described her as independent and insightful with an authentic and calm personality.

At the end of the house tour, Stella had looked out the window in the kitchen and noticed the garden in the back yard. Stella asked him if they could walk out to get a closer look. He watched Stella explore the overgrown and unkempt garden. She would reach down occasionally to touch the soil and feel the leaves. Stella's voice filled with excitement as she discovered hidden squash vines and tall stalks of asparagus. After that, he knew that Stella would be a great addition to the house and was thrilled to have someone who could bring life to the garden once more.

He chose Maggie as his third tenant. Like Davey, almost everyone on campus knew Maggie Mae. She was a full professor, department chairperson, and taught sociology, human development, and psychology. He always considered her to be strong and confident.

While viewing the house, Maggie had talked about playing in her band every Friday night at Frontier Brewery. He was impressed that she's able to play in front of large crowds. She had explained that she doesn't even think about it; she just loves to sing. She hadn't thought about being self-conscious. Stella and Maggie met at Frontier. Stella had overheard Maggie talking to her friends about needing a pad to rent, so she mentioned the place she was looking into, and the rest is history as they say.

The last tenant he chose was Rubin, who taught classes full time and worked part-time as an electrician at the college. With his skills, experience, and level of responsibility, it surprised Davey to learn that Rubin was still in his 20s. He had seen and talked with Rubin several times on campus over the past year. He noticed the lyrical way Rubin carried himself. Like every step was a beat from his own internal soundtrack. For him, the music never stopped.

He remembered standing on the front porch listening to the rumble of Rubin's motorcycle as he rode up the lane to the house. Rubin turned onto the drive and rolled past the front steps, turning his bike to the left and walking it backwards, closer to the porch. In a well-rehearsed rhythm, he flipped the ignition switch to off, kicked out the kick stand, and leaned the bike on its stand. As soon as the panhead engine went silent, Rubin threw his right leg over the rear fender, pivoted on his left foot and stood facing the porch. He greeted

Davey with a smile on his face and a sparkle in his eyes. He'd instinctively smiled back. Rubin's enthusiasm for life and adventure was contagious. This was not the first time he had been infected by Rubin's genuine zest and ease in which he approached life.

Davey removed the extra applications from the table, gazing happily at the magical four. He leaned back in his chair, satisfied and pleased with his choices for the four tenants.

He contacted the successful applicants, scheduled their move-in dates, and invited them to come over after their classes on Tuesday so he could show them their rooms. He also thought they might like to meet each other.

Tenant Application

Name: JOEY GARCIA _ _ _ _ _

Casper College:

Duration at the College: II YEARS _ _ _ _ _

Department: FINE ARTS _ _ _ _ _ _ _ _ _ _

Position: FULL PROFESSOR _ _ _ _ _ _ _ _

Personal Information:

Where did you grow up: BAY AREA - SAN FRANCISCO _ _

Education: MONTANA STATE UNIVERSITY _ _ _ _ _ _

How long have you lived in Casper: II YEARS _ _ _ _ _

Hobbies/Pastimes: WRITING POETRY TO RECITE AT LOCAL COFFEE SHOPS. I REALLY DIG GOING TO SCRAP YARDS TO FIND SOURCE MATERIAL FOR MY ARTWORK AND SCULPTURES. METAL IS KINDA _ MY THING.

Preferences:

Is personal hygiene important to you? (Yes) or No
BUT I DON'T JUDGE

Does noise bother you? Yes or (No)
DEPENDS ON THE NOISE

Do you prefer? (Coffee) or Tea

Do you like people? (Yes) or No
FOR THE MOST PART

Do people generally like you? (Yes) or No

Would you be okay with rural living? (Yes) or No
FOR THE MOST PART

Do you mind a 25 minute commute to work? Yes or (No)

Are you interested in car pooling? (Yes) or No
DEPENDS ON THE OCCUPANTS

Joey's Application

```
                    Tenant Application
Name: Stella Lesh _ _ _ _ _ _

Casper College:
    Duration at the College: Starting 5th year _

    Department: Science _ _ _ _ _ _ _ _ _ _

    Position: Associate Professor _ _ _ _ _ _
Personal Information:
    Where did you grow up: Jackson, Wyoming _ _ _ _ _ _

    Education: University of Washington. Master's in Chemistry, JD, MBA

    How long have you lived in Casper: 5 years _ _ _ _ _
```

Hobbies/Pastimes: While in Arizona, I had a greenhouse where I grew fruits and vegetables to sell at my fair trade store. I enjoy horticulture in general but specifically growing vegetables and herbs. Also like learning about other disciplines and researching other areas of science.

Preferences:

Is personal hygiene important to you? (Yes) or No

Does noise bother you? Yes or (No)   Not usually as long as the noise has a purpose

Do you prefer? (Coffee) or (Tea)   Mostly coffee but occasionally tea

Do you like people? (Yes) or No

Do people generally like you? (Yes) or No

Would you be okay with rural living? (Yes) or No

Do you mind a 25 minute commute to work? Yes or (No)

Are you interested in car pooling? (Yes) or No   No but I would need assistance with transportation

It would be delightful to share my commute with housemates.

Stella's Application

Tenant Application

Name: _Maggie Mae Mydland_

Casper College:

Duration at the College: _10 years_

Department: _Psychology_

Position: _Full Professor_

Personal Information:

Where did you grow up: _Rock Springs_

Education: _University of Wyoming and Univsity of Arizona_

How long have you lived in Casper: _10 years_

Hobbies/Pastimes: _I sing and play piano for a local band. We perform at Frontier on Friday nights. I also like fly fishing and hiking along the river looking for the elusive Wyoming Northern River Otter._

Preferences:

Is personal hygiene important to you? (Yes) or No

Cleanliness is next to Godliness

Does noise bother you? Yes or (No) _not usually but when I am trying to accomplish a task I like a more tranquil environmet_

Do you prefer? (Coffee) or Tea

Do you like people? (Yes) or No

Do people generally like you? (Yes) or No

Would you be okay with rural living? (Yes) or No

Do you mind a 25 minute commute to work? Yes or (No) _Living in the country would be refreshing_

Are you interested in car pooling? (Yes) or No

I could provide a vehicle for carpooling

Maggie's Application

```
                    Tenant Application
Name: Rubin Hart _ _ _ _ _ _ _

Casper College:
    Duration at the College: 8 months on and off _ _

    Department: Automotive Technology _ _ _ _ _ _ _

    Position: Instructor _ _ _ _ _ _ _ _ _ _ _ _ _

Personal Information:        Lived in Austin, Texas until I was 15 and then
    Where did you grow up: moved to Casper. Lived in Laramie for 18 months
                           to attend WyoTech. I've been back for about a year.

    Education: WyoTech- electrician and automotive technician _ _

    How long have you lived in Casper: About a year _ _ _

Hobbies/Pastimes: I like taking my Harley out on long rides throughout
_Wyoming. I enjoy working on anything that has an electrical ignition and/or a
combustible engine. I have always enjoyed taking things apart to see how they work.

Preferences:

    Is personal hygiene important to you?   (Yes)  or  No
                                               But people do get dirty
    Does noise bother you?   Yes  or (No)     working on things
                                    I love my loud bike
    Do you prefer?  (Coffee)  or  Tea

    Do you like people?   (Yes)  or  No  People are so wild, man

    Do people generally like you? (Yes) or No  I need my space and
                              I think so       fresh air to breathe
    Would you be okay with rural living?  (Yes)  or  No

    Do you mind a 25 minute commute to work?  Yes  or (No)

    Are you interested in car pooling?  (Yes) or  No
Any chance to ride my bike through the Wyoming countryside is cool with me. I'm
down with carpooling to work when the roads are bad.
```

Rubin's Application

3

CLAWFOOT TUB

"Communication Breakdown"
— Led Zeppelin

They started arriving late Tuesday afternoon. He greeted them at the door and showed them into the parlor where he had fresh coffee waiting. Once the group had assembled, he led them into the kitchen where he had the blueprints for the house laid out on the table. "Based on your applications, I've selected a room I think you'll like. One that fits your profile."

"My personal space is important to me. I'd like to take part in the decision," Maggie said.

"Wow, Wavey Davey, you've really put a lot of thought and consideration into designating the rooms. I know we saw them on our tours, but could you walk us through the rooms one more time?" added Stella.

"Yes, I'd like to see the rooms first," said Maggie.

"Something tells me that touring the rooms might be a good long-term investment for our peace and harmony," said Joey.

"Fair enough, let's go upstairs," said Rubin.

"Follow me," said Davey as he led them down the hall and up the stairs to the second floor.

Davey started the tour with the room immediately across from the landing. "This is Joey's room. The attached bathroom has a bathtub and shower, and there is a view of the lake from the bedroom that might be inspirational for his poetry and art."

Davey took them into the laundry room that was to their left. "As you can see, there's a utility sink. Rubin, this would be a great place for you since you like working on engines. When you come upstairs, you can clean up in this sink and toss your soiled coveralls into the washer. Your room is conveniently located next door. Here, let me show you."

He exited the laundry room and turned left to lead them into the space he had designated for Rubin. They walked inside and poked their heads into the closet and bathroom.

"Far out! This is one cool little space. I could do a lot with this," said Joey as he checked out the little sunroom that overlooked the front yard. "Hey Rubin, if possible could we switch rooms? I'd like space to do my art and have quick access to the utility sink in the laundry room to rinse out my brushes."

"I'm down with that. I dig all of those windows and natural light in the room across the hall. If no one else wants that room, swapping is cool with me," answered Rubin.

"Before we decide, I'd like to see all the rooms first," interjected Maggie.

"Wavey Davey, you were going to show us the other bedrooms..." added Stella.

Davey led them back to the hall and turned left past the staircase. After Maggie's recent concerns, he was nervous about showing the room he had designated as hers. He passed her doorway and led them into the room at the end of the hall.

"Through here is the bedroom I picked out for Stella." He turned to Stella and said, "I know you are a fairly private person so I gave you a little more space and a larger bathroom with a soaker tub."

"Thank you, Davey. That's very thoughtful," said Stella.

Maggie walked into the bathroom and saw the clawfoot tub. "What an exquisite view from this bathtub! I could spend hours reading and relaxing in here." She left the bathroom and explored the rest of the suite.

"Well, if you're ready, I'll show you the last bedroom," said Davey, leading them to the hall. He gestured to the right, "There is one extra room through there, but that doesn't have its own bathroom. It was a playroom when the girls were little." He walked back towards the stairs and motioned to the doorway on the left.

The others entered the room and explored. Davey waited in the hallway.

"Maggie, what do you think?" Joey asked.

"I'm okay with the two of you swapping rooms, if Stella is," said Maggie.

"That's groovy with me," said Stella. "Maggie, I wondered if you would like to take the room at the end of the hall that was designated for me?"

"Wow, yeah, I think that room would be perfect," answered Maggie.

"Are you sure, Stella?" said Davey. "That room seemed suited for you."

"Absolutely. I anticipate spending time in the garden and library," responded Stella.

"Outstanding! Sounds like we're all set," said Rubin.

"Awesome, man. I'm moving in first!" said Joey.

First floor of Davey's house

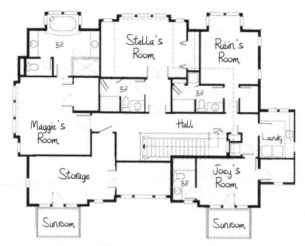

Second floor of Davey's house

That Saturday, Joey kept his word. By the following Friday evening, everyone had moved in. There they all were, sitting on the porch of the house, admiring the view of the mountains and sharing stories about their adventures and passions, especially for music. As the sun began to set, Davey looked around, amazed. So many different personalities! There they were: Davey, Joey, Stella, Maggie, and Rubin.

"What a group! Now this will be fun!" Davey did not realize that he had spoken his thought out loud until he saw the looks on everyone's faces.

There was a moment of silence and then Joey said, "Well Wavey Davey, thank you for saying it because we were all thinking it. At least, I know I was."

They smiled in agreement and broke into laughter.

4

UNPREDICTABLE HAIR

"Let It Rock"
— *Chuck Berry*

Now that the busy day had ended, the house became quiet again. All of Davey's guests were settled in, enjoying their new digs. He lounged in the library, sitting in his favorite green recliner and savoring a chocolate from his tin of Donells Candies. As he sat there, he couldn't help but smile. The day had been busy with new people and conversations about each person's passions and dreams. He found it both exciting and different with these strangers in his house.

Even though a week had passed since his first guest arrived, it was not until today that all of his empty rooms were fully occupied. He thought it was fun to see bedroom walls covered with Hendrix and Dylan posters and peace sign tapestries again. Even other areas in the house had more life. Maggie's two lava lamps and Rubin's white egg chair with orange lining enhanced the parlor. Stella's three potted plants sat in the kitchen windows, and Joey's large metal sculpture stood in the foyer. Someone had even wound the cuckoo clock. He figured that the amount of 8-tracks and albums in the house had quadrupled.

As usual, he sat alone, but for the first time in a very long while, this house, his house, had started to feel like a home again. He sat there feeling full of hope and confidence that the music would come back. He was not sure exactly what was creating these wonderful feelings, but he knew he felt them, and he knew he had not felt these feelings for over a year. He could not help but wonder if there was something new and exciting on the horizon for him and his tenants.

The next day was Saturday. During the night came the sound of thunder with the rain pouring down. The whole house slept, serenaded by the melody of the rain. This would be the first morning the group would be together. The rain stopped at daybreak and the sun began to shine. Davey had awoken early to start the coffee and put a kettle on the stove. The new tenants slowly emerged one by one. They hadn't discussed meeting in the kitchen, but it seemed natural to begin their day there. Perhaps they were drawn to the fragrance of breakfast cooking or the aroma of coffee brewing.

Each tenant walked in, casually greeted the others, and poured a cup of coffee or tea. Davey stood at the stove cooking while everyone else sat around the kitchen table. In a nook surrounded by windows, the large table could easily seat everyone comfortably. The morning sun shone into the nook providing a gentle warmth and glow.

Joey, with a coffee cup in his hand, got up from the table and walked over to the stove. "Breakfast smells great. What are you making?"

Davey looked up and smiled at Joey. "Just some eggs and bacon. I bet you have something more elaborate in mind. Do you want to take over while I get myself a cup of coffee?"

"Wow, really? Yeah man, I'd be happy to help!" Joey said.

"It's all yours. I have plenty of eggs and fresh vegetables in the fridge. Make anything you would like," Davey said as he walked over to the percolator and poured a fresh cup.

"It'll be groovy to grow our own vegetables," Stella added as she walked to the window that overlooked the garden. "It's such a wonderful experience to grow and nurture plants. It's peaceful to dig with your hands and let the soil run through your fingers."

The morning seemed to flow effortlessly. The menu for breakfast was a smorgasbord of smells. Joey seemed to be a master chef, able to make just about any request. Little did they know, weekend breakfast would become their routine. During the clean-up process, Stella asked Maggie about the crowd the night before at Frontier Brewery. Smiling, Maggie teased about how the crowd was kind because her band did not play their best show. This intrigued Joey. He said, "I'll be the judge of that! Let's go into the parlor and you can play us a few tunes."

With a little more encouragement, Maggie led the group into the parlor and sat down at the piano. She fidgeted with the keys, pensively playing a few scales.

"Come on, let it ride," said Joey.

Maggie looked up and said, "It's much harder playing in an intimate setting like this."

Stella said, "Don't sweat it. I've heard you play several times at Frontier. You're phenomenal."

Maggie smiled, closed her eyes, and began to play. No longer tentative, her fingers floated along the keys and the sound of "Kozmic Blues" filled the air. Absorbing the music, she swayed to the melody, her shoulders rising and falling with the rhythm.

"I'm really digging what you're putting down. You know what this sound needs?" Rubin said.

"An upright bass," replied Stella.

"Electric guitar," said Joey.

"Yes, and it needs a backbeat," said Rubin.

Maggie paused and added, "Groovy, let's jam!"

"All right, everybody fetch your instruments and meet back here in five minutes," said Davey.

"So, Wavey Davey, we're gonna meet back here?" Joey said with a grin and a wink.

Rubin came back with his bongo. Stella had her upright bass. Joey had his electric guitar. Davey came back with his acoustic guitar. Maggie played a tune, and the others joined in. In the middle of the song, Maggie began singing in such a beautiful and soulful voice that everyone almost stopped in surprise. The richness and emotion of her voice was mesmerizing, like a well-heated lava lamp. Stella began tapping her feet, and before anyone knew it, she broke into a dynamic jazz riff on her upright bass. This was such a contrast to the quiet and reserved personality they were getting used to that Joey said, "That's one funky beat! I dig it."

As the band continued to play, Joey spontaneously joined Maggie in singing. His husky but melodic voice blended with hers. The housemates looked at each other, smiled and nodded in satisfaction. They jammed all morning and into the afternoon. It quickly became clear that the sound they were creating was something they wanted to preserve. They decided to begin writing it down as they created their own new collaborative sound.

"Whoa, it's almost dinner time!" said Davey, looking at the cuckoo clock.

"Oh yeah, now that you mention it, I'm pretty hungry," said Joey.

"Dinner sounds good to me. To the kitchen!" said Rubin.

"I wonder what we have that can be made quickly so we can get back to jamming," said Maggie as they walked toward the kitchen.

Davey opened cabinets and Stella checked the refrigerator. "Well, we have a few tins of SPAM," said Davey. "We can make fried SPAM sandwiches."

"We can top them with lettuce and tomato," added Stella.

"I bought some cheddar Snack Mate cheese at Sloanes General Store. We can use that too," said Joey.

"What's that?" asked Maggie.

"It's a can of spray cheese. It's fun! Like Cheez Whiz, only sprayable," said Joey.

"Huh, sounds interesting," said Maggie. "I do like Cheez Whiz sandwiches."

Rubin sliced the SPAM and Davey fried the slices. Stella and Maggie cut fresh juicy tomatoes and chopped the lettuce. Joey created hors d'oeuvres with the cheddar Snack Mate, RITZ crackers, and some crumbled up bacon from breakfast. Rubin opened the cans of Whistles and Bugles. When the SPAM was finished, everyone made a sandwich and enjoyed the other snacks.

Rubin grabbed a Bugle and filled it with Snack Mate cheese. He tossed it in his mouth and grinned with delight, "Far out man. Fun food."

Maggie picked up the Snack Mate cheese, tilted the can, and depressed the nozzle to fill a Whistle. Cheese shot out quickly and soon overflowed the salty corn snack. "Fun and tasty!"

Everyone laughed and joined in to make their own creations with the cheese and other eatable items. They had fun experimenting with their food.

After a much-needed break for dinner, they returned to the parlor to keep jamming. After a few hours, everyone was exhausted and excited as they slowly broke off and retired to bed. Little did they know, this was the beginning of their great adventure and future as a band.

As the warm days faded into the crispness of fall, the group played every night for hours on end. Before everyone knew it, they had a routine of playing in the parlor each night after they finished grading assignments and preparing the next day's lectures. Maggie and Stella created a cozy office complete with a large cherry desk, an orange table, and a blue and yellow floral recliner in the storage room on the second floor. They painted the room sunshine yellow and lime green. Joey brought in a tie-dyed tapestry to hang on the wall. Maggie hung a string of crystals in the windows of the sunroom, spiraling rainbows around. Stella brought in a suitcase record player and a few jazz albums to play softly in the background while they worked. Joey would pop in periodically to ask when they'd be ready to jam.

One Saturday morning in early September, Maggie came to the breakfast table with some exciting news. She had spoken to Betty, the stage manager at Frontier Brewery, and mentioned that she was now a member in another band. To her surprise, she offered to give them a gig for Saturday night.

"That's tonight!" exclaimed Stella with a touch of anxiety in her voice.

Rubin instantly replied, "Far out, I'm in a band! This is my first band."

"Well, apparently, we're all in a band," said Joey.

Davey wondered if the group was ready for such a big step. He glanced at Joey and Stella and it looked like they were thinking the same thing. Davey spoke up and asked the group if they wanted to vote on taking the gig. Everyone nodded in agreement.

Davey said, "All in favor of taking the gig tonight raise your hand."

Without hesitation, Davey raised his hand. He thought to himself, why not, it would be fun to play with his friends. It was the first time, he realized, that he considered his tenants to be his friends. Gradually, fearful looks turned to smiles of excitement and adventure. The vote was over. They decided to go for it! They all hurried to get their instruments so they could practice.

When evening rolled around, they were nervous but ready to play their first gig. They loaded all of their equipment and headed to Frontier Brewery. They walked in and looked at the stage.

"I didn't realize the stage would be this small," said Davey.

"Yep, it's always cozy up there," said Maggie. "We need to start with setting up the drum kit and then position the amps."

"I don't think my whole kit will fit," said Rubin. "I'll just play with my five-piece set."

"Okay, let's get everything unloaded and set up," said Joey. "We'll just have to figure it out as we go."

They began arranging the stage so that all the instruments, sound equipment, and band members could fit. Once the band had everything in place, they stood back and stared at the stage.

"We will be crammed in there like a bunch of sardines, trying to play," said Joey.

Hearing this, Stella looked at the expressions on the other faces and saw that Davey and Rubin were also concerned. "Hey, it'll be like playing Twister," she said to lighten the mood.

"I have played here many times, and it's not as bad as it looks. Let's get tuned up and ready for our show," said Maggie. "We're going to start with setting the volume levels in the monitors. Then we'll set up the amps. Trust me, this show will be far out."

Joey slung his guitar over his shoulder and plugged in. He waited for the usual pop of confirmation from the amp. Nothing happened. "Does anyone else have power?"

The other members played a few notes to check their levels and sure enough, they all had sound. Joey adjusted the volume knob on his guitar and strummed again. There wasn't any sound coming from his amp. Joey checked the cable from his guitar to the amp and confirmed that it was connected.

Davey, noticing that the power light on the amp was not on, said, "Rubin, can you check to see if Joey's amp is plugged in?"

Sure enough, it was unplugged. Rubin informed Davey, "The cord is too short to reach the outlet. I'll run out to the truck and get another extension cord."

Rubin returned a minute later with a disappointed look on his face. "Cats, I hate to tell you this, but we don't have any more extension cords."

"Ask Betty if she has an extra one we can borrow," said Maggie.

Thankfully, she had cords, cables, and other extras that bands tend to forget but need to perform at her venue. They were able to finish tuning and set volume levels without any further mishaps.

The band started the show with Chuck Berry's "Let It Rock," followed by Janis Joplin's "Try (Just a Little Bit Harder)." The band and the crowd were having fun and enjoying the evening. During, "Get Off of My Cloud," Joey in his exuberance nearly knocked Davey off the stage. Joey quickly grabbed Davey's elbow and pulled him away from the edge. They had a few missteps and wrong notes, but it didn't matter because the crowd kept dancing and loving the music.

During "Roll Over Beethoven," Davey, a little rattled from nearly falling off the stage, tripped over the cord in front of Stella's upright bass and knocked the microphone stand onto Rubin's drum kit. Rubin instinctively stood up, caught the microphone stand with one hand, continued playing with the other, and smoothly pushed the stand back into place. He sat back down and kept drumming, never missing a beat. Davey grinned at him and kept rocking.

Most of the audience stayed until closing time. The band was really getting into a groove, but the owner of Frontier Brewery had to shut the show down. It bummed them to stop jamming, but it was time to go. It had been a long night of playing.

Back at the house, they were so jazzed that they couldn't sleep. They were still full of energy and excitement from the show. They were officially a band now that they'd played their first gig. A band without a name, but a band just the same. Davey asked Joey what he was trying to communicate during

"Smokestack Lightnin'" when he nodded back to Rubin.

"That tells me we're making the transition from the solo back to the main rhythm of the song. I change the beat and Stella starts the progression," Rubin said.

"Yeah, then the next time I hear that bass rhythm, I start singing," Joey said.

"Good gravy, I just realized that I automatically follow that progression without even thinking about it," Davey said.

"I wasn't sure if the crowd was digging the second set at first," added Maggie. "I started 'Hey Jude' and the crowd went silent. Thankfully, the rest of you jumped in and started grooving. I knew we were really making something special when the crowd sang the final chorus."

"It was beautiful when we stopped playing and the crowd kept singing," said Stella.

The next morning, Davey slept in later than usual because he was not accustomed to such late nights. Davey entered the kitchen around 9 a.m. and saw his bandmates sitting around the breakfast table in various states of exhaustion.

He soon noticed that something was missing. The expected aroma of coffee and bacon was absent. It was obvious that the group didn't get much sleep. They were drinking orange Tang since that required little effort to mix into cold water. They were wearing the threads they'd worn to the show the night before, and their hair indicated they'd just woken up.

Maggie's blond hair, usually well kept, was flat on one side and sticking up on the other. Every strand of Joey's hair seemed to stand up at crazy angles. Stella's bangs were flat, and the rest of her hair was full of static electricity. Even the hair in Rubin's goatee was pointing in seven directions.

"Goodness, you all look like a bunch of bed heads!" said Davey as he poured himself a glass of water and stirred in a spoonful of powdered Tang.

One by one, they lifted their heads from the table like prairie dogs popping up from their holes. A minute of silence passed as they looked around the table at each other. That's when the giggling started, a slow eruption with Maggie's quiet snickers at the epicenter. The laughter gained momentum, increasing each time anyone made eye contact. It reached its peak when Joey snorted. Now they were all laughing. Some to the point of tears.

Davey was right, they did look like a bunch of bed heads. The name seemed to fit.

"That's it, bro! We should call ourselves The Bed Heads!" Rubin said.

"The Bed Heads," said Stella, wiping her eyes. "I like it."

They all raised their cups and toasted, "The Bed Heads!"

5

MIND EXPLOSION

"Playing in the Band"
— Grateful Dead

Their first gig had been an astounding experience. The Bed Heads were an official band with an official name! The group continued with their jam sessions at the house each evening. Every member contributed to the band's musical identity. The more the band played together, the better they became at picking up on each other's cues and transitions from the verses to the chorus. Joey would give a little nod to Maggie and make eye contact with Rubin just before he launched into a solo on his guitar. Rubin knew that meant he was to play a constant beat to guide Joey's riffs and support the rhythms of the other band members.

The only room more popular than the kitchen was the parlor, which had the perfect atmosphere for sound exploration. Joey, finishing a particularly Chuck Berry-esque solo, propped his guitar against the walnut console, paused, and flipped the lid open. "Wait a second, this plays cassettes? Man, it looks brand new. Have you ever used this?" said Joey.

"My wife and I were only able to play it a couple of times," Davey said.

Stella walked over to take a look. "Does it have a record player?"

"That's a solid-state system! It doesn't just play records. It plays records in Hi-Fi stereo," Rubin said.

"And apparently cassettes," said Joey.

"I don't have cassettes, but I have several Hi-Fi albums," Maggie said.

"I'm not sure if they're Hi-Fi, but I definitely have a lot of records," Stella said.

"I noticed all of you had crates of records when you moved in. You guys should use this some time," Davey said.

"Some time? Let's fire this thing up now," Joey said.

They disappeared and came back carrying full record crates. Maggie suggested that each person pull out their top five favorite albums. Rubin looked over at Stella's stack, noticed her copy of "Sketches of Spain," and said, "Miles Davis!" He smiled and held up "Miles in The Sky."

"That is a good one. It's a little too hyper for me with all the different sounds happening at once. I prefer the harmonious rhythms on here," Stella said, pointing to her album.

Maggie put on Herbie Hancock's "Maiden Voyage." As Herbie's piano played in the background, she said, "So my five include this glorious piece by Herbie Hancock, 'Surrealistic Pillow' by Jefferson Airplane, 'Ella in Hamburg' by Ella Fitzgerald, 'Showcase' by Patsy Cline, and a new self-titled release by Big Brother and the Holding Company featuring Janis Joplin."

"Thanks, Maggie. We appreciate your enthusiastic sharing. Stella, you were saying?" Joey said.

"Well, Miles Davis," gesturing to the album in her hand. She added it back to the crate and held up John Coltrane's "Coltrane Jazz," then Charlie Parker's "Bird is Free," and finally Merle Haggard's "Mama Tried."

"Play that one!" said Joey, pointing to the Merle Haggard record.

"Here, I'll put it on," Maggie said.

"Alright I'll start out with Miles Davis as well," Rubin said, holding up "Miles in the Sky." He set the record on the floor and picked up "My Generation" by The Who. "I really dig Keith Moon on this album, especially during the title track. Another favorite is from Creedence Clearwater Revival. And Carlos Santana. My absolute favorite, though, is this debut Grateful Dead record."

"Big Brother and the Holding Company, man. I saw them at the Monterey Pop Festival. I'd like to listen to that one too," said Joey.

"You were there?" said Davey. "My friend, Bear, and I couldn't make that show, but we went to San Francisco later. Can you believe we ran into two people in The Haight from Wyoming? They had something to do with that band, the grateful whatever you just mentioned. One was named Bob or Bobby and the other guy was one of the Barlow boys from Pinedale."

"What a small world," said Maggie, taking the next record out of its sleeve.

"Speaking of the Monterey Pop Festival, this guy is the world's best guitar player," Joey said, holding up 'Are You Experienced' by The Jimi Hendrix Experience. "I wish I had a live recording of his performance at Monterey, but I haven't been able to get my hands on one yet. So, this," holding up 'Electric Ladyland,' "is the best Jimi Hendrix record I know of in existence. Now, a live album from another legend is 'Chuck Berry in London'. Okay, Buddy Guy. Brilliant dude. He's going to be a legend someday for sure," pointing to 'A Man and the Blues.' "Another unbelievable band with an incredible guitarist, Eric Clapton and Cream. Now, this album will blow your mind. I've spun 'The White Album' by The Beatles so many times it's wearing a groove."

"My girls wore out all of our Elvis Presley albums. I can't tell you how many times I've heard 'Hound Dog' and 'Jailhouse Rock.' Seems like every time I went to play Bill Monroe and the Blue Grass Boys, I'd find an Elvis record," said Davey. "I have this new Neil Young album. He was in Buffalo Springfield and it looks like he's on his own for now. The first track is an instrumental about Wyoming."

"How fun, a song about our illustrious state. Let's play it," said Maggie.

"That cover is far out. I mean, the symbolism of the mountains and the city skyline being inverted or like a reflection of each other is too cool," said Joey.

"I dig how the cover doesn't have any words, like a title or anything," reflected Stella, "That's a powerful statement. The cover and the music inside speak for themselves."

"Just like the first track on the album. No words, just music. Beautiful continuation of the artwork. I love it," said Joey.

Over the next few weeks the band expanded their collaboration. They tried different sounds and gave each band member a turn at expressing their musical style and talents. The band became so in tune with each other's style of playing that they were all able to improvise by allowing each member to step up and share in playing a solo. Joey's and

Maggie's voices melted together as they sang. The other members joined in to harmonize during the chorus. They continued to write songs and explore sounds influenced by each other's favorite musicians. Each member seemed to have a deep and sincere love for music, as evidenced by the size and variety of their combined vinyl collection.

The band developed a diverse repertoire of songs. They had an awesome collective talent for writing music and lyrics. The beauty of the group, which became their unspoken mantra, was that everyone had a voice and experiences that, when brought together, created the band's sound. Everyone had something to bring to the sound they were creating. Because of this mantra, all of the band members enjoyed the freedom of contributing to the lyrics and music. In fact, they encouraged each other to experiment with sounds and share their ideas. The music was exciting and full of energy! They blended the influences of blues, folk, rock, bluegrass, jazz, Americana, country, and Latin into their own unique style, rhythm, and music. As they played, their individual notes fused into a stream of melodious sound.

As each member explored his or her talents and passion areas, their roles sort of evolved as the band developed their own musical content. It was cool how Maggie and Joey became the primary writers for the lyrics, while Davey, Stella, and Rubin developed many of the musical arrangements. As the band wrote songs and practiced cover tunes, each member explored new instruments.

Stella usually played the upright bass, but she started learning the electric. She borrowed an electric bass from a student at the college to try it out in a couple of jam sessions and explore how to generate different sounds. She liked the ability to create deep rich tones with one strum and then get a lighter airier melody with the next. Stella learned to drive and lead the band during certain parts of the song, and to support the band members with rhythm during other parts. She loved the diversity and flexibility the electric bass gave her.

Davey had always played the acoustic guitar. He learned on an acoustic when he was growing up on the ranch in Ten Sleep, Wyoming. When he and his family would go on road trips, the girls would request songs for him to play around the campfire at night. As he played, the family would join in singing westerns, American folk, and their favorite rock 'n' roll songs. The family would spend hours around the fire, singing and telling stories about their current adventure, and dreaming about adventures to come.

One day while taking a break during a jam session, Davey thought about the different sounds of the electric and acoustic guitar. Sitting alone with Joey in the parlor, he asked, "Have you always played electric guitar?"

"No, I actually used to only play acoustic, but one day my friend left his electric guitar and amp at my house. Out of curiosity, I picked it up and started playing. I remember hearing the pop of the amp as I turned it on," Joey said with a smile as he motioned a pop with his hands. "I knew this was something totally new and cool."

With a look of mesmerized awe on his face and in his eyes, Joey continued, "I was hooked, brother. I mean, I just closed my eyes as I felt the vibration of the first E string. Then A. Then D. The sound just reverberated through my mind, down to my fingers and into my soul. It completely blew my mind." He held his closed left hand to the side of his head and then opened his fingers slowly and pulled his hand away, gesturing the explosion of his mind.

"Wavey Davey, you have to try the electric guitar, man." Joey said excitedly as he held out his electric Gibson SG Standard cherry with black pickguard.

"This is such a beautiful guitar," Davey said as he took the guitar and held it in almost complete amazement. He put the strap over his shoulder and adjusted the position of the guitar. He turned and grabbed the pick stuck in the strings at the top fret of his acoustic. "I'm shaking a bit," he said, looking over at Joey who was now standing about three feet away. Joey just nodded and smiled with kind reassurance. "Here it goes," Davey said as he gripped his pick and strummed the strings with gentle precision.

"Now really strum it," Joey encouraged with enthusiasm by gesturing an intense full body strum with his 'air guitar.' "Let it rip, man. Feel the vibration."

Davey took a breath and pulled his arm into the air above his head. As Davey dropped his arm into a furious strum, he closed his eyes and leaned back in anticipation of the explosion that was soon to follow. As Davey's pick hit the strings, the stack of Marshall speakers detonated in a wave of sound. Davey paused for a second to feel the waves surge through his body. They seemed to resonate in the marrow of his bones and cascade into the center of his chest. His face was full of the absolute thrill he felt in his heart as he opened his eyes and played a tune.

"You have just been turned on to the sound of the electric wonder land," Joey proclaimed with joy and admiration. He put his arm around Davey's shoulder. "Welcome to rock 'n roll my friend. It feels good, doesn't it?"

Gesturing toward the other band members as they entered the parlor, he told Davey, "See, the magical power of the electric guitar has called out to our friends and guided them home again."

"That was Wavey Davey wailing on the guitar? Far out," Rubin said.

"Let's finish our session and then get Wavey Davey to Rockstar Music Store so he can get himself a new guitar," Joey said.

"A new electric guitar," Davey corrected with excitement.

"Absolutely," exclaimed Rubin, "forget finishing the jam session. Let's get Wavey Davey to Rockstar now."

"Stella, are you ready to commit to an electric bass?" asked Maggie with an encouraging smile. "I know you have been borrowing one, but do you think it's time to get your own?"

"Wow, yeah. I think I might be ready. That'd give us more room on stage at Frontier," said Stella. "I've been looking at a Fender with a sunburst finish for a few weeks down at the shop. I've put some money away in case I wanted to get it."

"It would be great to have fewer hazards on stage. For safety. Or at least, my safety," Davey said.

"That's right, Wavey Davey," said Maggie.

Joey winked at Davey and added, "Yeah, agreed. No more hazards on stage. I'm stoked about the potential for our new electrified sound."

They got their jackets and headed to Rockstar Music Store.

"I've always dug this Fender Strat guitar neck door handle. It never gets old," Joey said as he pulled the door open.

Davey veered to the left towards the line of acoustic guitars hanging on the wall. As he reached for the Martin in the middle, Joey interrupted, "I think what you're looking for is on the other wall. Come on, let's get your hands on a Les Paul."

Joey led him over to the opposite wall, which was full of electric guitars. They held an improvisational jam session to help their bandmates try out different instruments. Davey and Stella picked out their new guitars. Stella got her starburst Fender and Davey bought a Les Paul Goldtop.

Before heading back to Alcova, Davey took them down the street to Donells Candies, his favorite chocolate shop. Davey explained, "I'm getting a bag of Dark Chocolate Pecan Clusters. My wife and I used to buy them here. She'd put half of the bag in a piece of Tupperware in the kitchen and I'd fill the tin on my desk in the library with the other half."

"So, what you're saying is that there are chocolates hidden in the Tupperware in the kitchen?" Joey said with a smirk.

"Probably," said Davey.

"Groovy!" said Stella as she walked farther into the shop.

"I can't believe I haven't been here! I've lived here most of my life," Maggie said while gazing at the display case full of fudge, brittles, truffles, chocolates, toffees, and barks.

Davey bought his chocolates. Rubin picked up a box of Milk Chocolate Mint Patties, Stella bought Chocolate Dipped Strawberries, Maggie chose Dark Chocolate Cashew Mavericks, and Joey purchased English Toffee.

Next, they made an impromptu stop at Wind City Books to grab coffee and reading material. They fanned out inside the store to explore the shelves. Stella searched for a book about the chemical compounds of diesel fuel. Rubin picked up a book about engine repair. Joey found a book in the Staff Picks section by new author, Jack Kerouac. They made their purchases and headed back on the road.

6

FREE CHILI

"Weather Report Suite, Part 2 (Let It Grow)"
— Grateful Dead

It was a beautiful, crisp Wednesday morning in the fall. Engaging conversation and the scent of coffee filled the air. Stella walked in, smiled, and proudly set a pumpkin on the kitchen table. "Our first fruit from the garden! I found this beauty when I was cleaning up outside. I've been nurturing it ever since."

"I knew that garden still had life. It just needed to be loved by a groovy care taker," Maggie said.

"Right on! I can't wait until we have more pumpkins for carving jack-o'-lanterns," said Rubin.

"After we carve the pumpkins, we can roast the seeds," said Maggie.

"That is so cool how a pumpkin can be used in different ways," Rubin said.

"My wife planted several types of fruits and vegetables. It's nice to know that some of what she started still grows," added Davey. "When the girls were little, we started growing carving pumpkins to make jack-o'-lanterns. Then we grew sugar pumpkins because my wife liked to bake pies."

Maggie put her hand on Davey's shoulder and said, "Far out, this garden was really an important part of your family. I didn't even know there were different types of pumpkins."

"It's beautiful that we can continue the legacy of your wife and family," Joey said before taking his last bite of toast.

"I found a sugar pumpkin that's almost ripe enough to pick. I can't wait until we can bake a pie," said Stella, walking over to the stove to start a fresh cup of tea.

Rubin looked at his watch and rose from his seat. "I should pack my lunch."

Maggie and Joey followed suit, clearing their plates. Joey started washing the dishes while Maggie dried. Stella walked slowly across the kitchen, blowing on the steaming cup of tea she was cradling in both hands. She noticed that Davey had pulled the pumpkin closer to him. He stared quietly at it. Stella carefully sat down on the bench and gently placed her cup on the table.

She looked up and saw the moisture that had formed in Davey's eyes. She could tell that he was transfixed in a memory awakened by the familiar orange fruit. He reached out and gently caressed the pumpkin as if he were touching the face of a loved one. Stella placed her hand on Davey's forearm. His gaze did not shift as he slowly brushed dirt from the pumpkin's base. After a few seconds, he looked at Stella while avoiding eye contact. "I think about her so much. Sometimes I forget that she is never coming home. I have to remind myself that she is not away visiting the girls. I have to remind myself that she is gone."

"I am sorry for bringing all this pain back for you," Stella said.

"It's not you. You have done a wonderful job bringing life back to the garden," Davey said, turning his head to look her in the eyes. "Thank you."

Stella smiled and nodded.

The wall phone rang, and as usual, Maggie was the first to answer. Betty, the stage manager at Frontier Brewery, was on the line. She was calling to let her know that a spot had opened in the schedule for Friday night. "If you want the gig, you'd get dibs before any other band. It's the annual chili contest at the brewery. This will be a bigger show with a packed audience."

Maggie put her hand over the handset, turned to the others, and repeated the offer. "I'd like to say yes. What do you think?"

"Absolutely," Rubin said. "We are a band, aren't we? Bands play gigs."

"I hope we get free chili," Joey said with a laugh. "I'm amped up for this! Let's play the show."

Stella chuckled. "Last time was so much fun. I vote that we take the gig. With or without the free chili."

Davey looked around the room at his fellow band members. "It looks like we're all in agreement. Maggie, please tell her that we will gladly fill in."

Maggie laughed and put the phone back up to her ear. "We'll do it! Add us to Friday night's lineup."

Betty said, "That's great! Please thank the rest of the band for helping me out. I'll see you on Friday night."

Maggie hung up the phone and refilled her coffee. The Bed Heads had their second gig in a month! Things were moving quickly.

Each of the band members gradually left the kitchen. Rubin was the first to leave for work since he had to be at the college for a 9:00 class. The others heard his Harley roar to life before he started down the drive to the main road.

Friday evening rolled around, and the band headed to Frontier Brewery to set up for their gig. The band gathered on the small stage, each pointing out where their equipment would best fit.

"Tell the truth, who's going to miss my upright bass?" Stella joked.

Davey laughed and said, "I can't wait to hear you play that Fender. That small Fender."

"Let's put Rubin's drums centered in the back. Stella's amp to his left. My keyboard in the front right. Joey in the center. And Davey just ahead of Stella," Maggie said.

"We can make that work," Joey said.

Rubin had just finished adjusting the heads on his drum kit when Betty walked up to the front of the stage. "The Bed Heads?" she said, pointing to the face of his bass drum.

"Isn't it nifty? We thought of the name after the last gig, and Joey painted the logo yesterday," explained Maggie. "We discussed the color and style and all agreed to use black block letters."

"Cool, it's unique and I like it. The Bed Heads," Betty said while raising her hands in the air as if pointing to a marque. "I can see your name in lights!"

The band finished setting up and tuning as the crowd arrived. They retired backstage, anxiously waiting for the stage lights to turn on so they could start the show. This was the first time the band would get to hear their name announced to an audience. With five minutes to go, they stood backstage and ran through the setlist one more time. As Betty dimmed the lights and took the stage, they gathered in a circle and encouraged each other to have fun and enjoy the jam. Finally, she announced, "Frontier Brewery presents Casper's newest and hottest band, The Bed Heads!"

The band opened their set with a rocking rendition of "Smokestack Lightnin'" followed by "Johnny B. Goode." By the time they got to "I Shall Be Released," the band was really getting into a groove. Maggie's eyes were closed as her fingers glided over the keys. Joey and Davey were facing each other, taking turns with riffs. Stella and Rubin kept a steady rhythm. The crowd was laughing, dancing, and singing as the music was swinging. The band and the crowd were lost in the moment.

Before they knew it, Betty stepped onstage to encourage them to take an intermission. Using Joey's mic, she told the audience, "Last chance to vote for your favorite chili! I'll be back in 10 minutes to announce the winner."

Turning to face the band, she said, "Great set so far! No one has tripped over a mic or almost fallen off the stage. Yet."

They all laughed in agreement.

"There's still time. We have a second set," said Joey.

Rubin and Davey made the rounds to the contestants and taste tested all of their contest entries. Maggie, having already been a regular performer at Frontier Brewery, was stopped by her fans as she left the stage. Stella and Joey followed Rubin and Davey. They tried several of the chilis and asked for recipes from the folks who made their favorites.

Annual Chili Cook-Off

[1]They headed back to the stage and Rubin played a ceremonial drumroll for Betty's big announcement. "And the winner of Frontier Brewery's chili contest is... John Barlow!"

---

1 Special thanks to Holland Hume of Geeks Who Drink for the glorious Jell-O graphic.

John came onto the stage to take a bow as the crowd applauded and cheered. Then The Bed Heads kicked off their second set with a red-hot rendition of "Not Fade Away."

Just like before, they kept playing until closing time. Unlike before, there weren't any mishaps. As the crowd dispersed, the band packed up and headed home. They were excited, yet exhausted, after such a fantastic evening that they didn't even bother to unload their gear. Everyone retired to their rooms, feeling satisfied that their second gig was so much fun.

7

MOBILE RAINBOW

"On the Road Again"
— *Willie Nelson*

A few days later, the phone rang. Rubin answered and said, "Hello, home of The Bed Heads, Rubin speaking."

It was Betty, the stage manager at Frontier Brewery. "Home of The Bed Heads. I love it! I've reached the right place then."

She explained that her friend, who was the organizer of a local music festival, had called looking for a band that could fill an empty slot in the festival lineup. Her friend asked if she knew any bands that could perform at the festival in short notice. Of course, she immediately thought of The Bed Heads. "I promised I'd call you and then call him back

ASAP. What do you think? You guys want to do your first music festival?"

Rubin put his hand over the handset and began to relay what she'd said. Davey quickly said, "Hey, my friend, Bear, installed this new device on the wall phone. Just push that little button on the base and she will be able to talk to all of us at once."

Rubin pushed the button on the side of the wall phone's base and said, "Hey Betty, can you hear us?"

"Loud and clear!"

"Far out! Wow, this is way cool, man!" said Rubin. "It's like being on stage and talking to the audience through the microphone."

Stella kindly interjected, "Betty, you were telling Rubin about something?"

"Yeah, there's an open slot in a festival lineup and I wondered if The Bed Heads would like to fill it," she replied.

Rubin smiled and with a look of "why not" of his face, gave a thumbs-up to the group.

"A music festival!" said Davey. "It's been a long time since I've been to one of those. I love music festivals in Wyoming. Bands from across the country play and—"

"Well, what do we want to do?" Maggie interrupted.

"Let's do it," Stella said.

"Yeah, let's do it," Davey agreed.

"I'm in," Joey said.

"You know I'm in," Rubin added.

"Great, let's do this. Our first touring gig!" Maggie said.

Rubin said, "Did you hear that? I think you have yourself a band for the festival. We'll do it!"

Betty explained that she would get the details from her friend and share them with the band later that day. Rubin hung up the phone and looked at the group.

"A festival," said Stella in a curiously nervous tone.

"Wow, this is a big step," said Joey.

"A huge step," agreed Davey. "Are we ready for this?"

"It's an adventure," Rubin said. "We're always ready for that."

"Agreed," Maggie said confidently.

"It will be great! Our first road trip," said Davey with a renewed sense of excitement for the coming adventure.

She called back about an hour later stating that she had contacted her friend and everything was set. This time Davey answered the phone and wrote down the details about the gig. As Davey hung up, Rubin said, "Well, every band has to hit the road at some point and now is our time."

"Road Trip!" Davey said with excitement. "I LOVE road trips!"

The group laughed because this was the most enthusiasm Davey had shown. They'd thought his level of excitement had peaked when he'd bought his new electric guitar. Davey explained to the group that he and his family had road tripped to the festival multiple times over the past 20 years. He talked about how the festival was a great place for the band to play and be heard by an awesome crowd. With that endorsement, the band members checked their schedules and agreed that they would leave for the festival on Saturday morning after breakfast.

Later that evening, Davey sat in his favorite green recliner in the library, enjoyed a Donells chocolate, and reflected on the day. This would be their first road trip and their first festival. Wow, they had a real show with a paying audience. He thought about the audience and wondered if they would like the music. He quickly settled into the idea that the band's energy would carry from the stage, infecting the audience with positive vibes. He smiled and embraced the renewed sense of joy. He was beginning to realize that this joy was cascading into his experiences, his relationships, and most of all, his life. He closed his eyes and let the joy fill his spirit, all the way to the marrow of his soul.

After breakfast on Saturday, the band members brought their instruments down to the front porch. They quickly ran through Maggie's checklist of the equipment to make sure that they hadn't forgotten anything. Unlike their Frontier Brewery gigs, this time they needed to bring all of their instruments as well as all of their sound equipment. As the band members waited for Davey on the porch, they talked about how they were nervous and excited about the gig. A few minutes later, Davey walked onto the porch, looked at all of their instruments and gear, and asked, "How are we going to get all of this to the festival?"

The band had a rainbow of vehicles. Rubin had a red Harley-Davidson motorcycle and an orange International Harvester Scout. Davey had a yellow Ford F100 pickup truck. Stella had a green bicycle. Maggie had a blue BMW 1500 4-door sedan. Joey had a purple VW bus. As usual, they would have to take more than one vehicle to get the instruments, gear, and band members to the show. They loaded the sound gear into Davey's truck and put the instruments into Joey's VW mini-bus. Davey drove his truck, Joey drove his VW, and the rest of the band members rode with Maggie in her 1500.

Traveling was long and slow as Joey's bus topped out at 55 mph. When they stopped for gas, Davey huddled the band together and informed them that, at their current rate of travel, they were going to arrive close to the start of the show. They wouldn't have much time to set up and tune.

Maggie said, "My keyboard doesn't need to be tuned. Rubin, I think you've tightened the heads on your drums and they just need minor adjustments. So, really, the only tuning that needs to happen is Stella's bass and Joey's and Davey's guitars. Okay so Rubin, you drive Joey's mini-bus since you can drive a stick shift. I'll drive Davey's pickup truck since it's an automatic. Davey, you drive my BMW and Joey and Stella will ride with you. Grab your guitars out of the mini-bus and tune them on the way to the festival."

"Well, Maggie, I couldn't tune my guitar if I was driving my truck or the BMW," said Davey.

"Yeah, that's a good point," Maggie said.

Stella said, "Maggie, it'll still work the way you have it planned. While he drives, Joey and I will tune Davey's guitar so that it sounds the way he likes it. Okay, I think we're ready to go."

They followed Maggie's plan and made it to the festival about 30 minutes before they were supposed to be onstage. They met briefly on the side of the stage and agreed to put drums in the back center, bass on the left, keyboard on the right, and guitars in the front center. The band quickly setup their sound equipment and instruments. The lights came on and the band was stunned at the size of the crowd. They looked nervously at each other.

our 1st festival!

Stella said, "Wow, there are a lot of people out there."

They all nodded in agreement. Davey quickly said, "All right, we're all anxious. We've got a lot of energy to use here. Let's channel this energy into our music and send great vibes into the crowd."

Rubin agreed with a nod. With a big smile on his face and his drumsticks held high in the air, he tapped out one, two, three, four. The band launched into their opening song. The energy of the music hit the crowd like a rushing wave. As the music washed over the crowd, they erupted into cheers and applause. By the third song in their set, the crowd was dancing and swaying, full of positive vibes.

For the first time, the band could feel the power of the crowd's energy flowing back to the stage. As the band felt the excitement from the crowd, they began to relax and their sound unfolded into a free-form experience. Instead of playing each song exactly as they'd rehearsed, they experimented with the instrumental sections. As they explored new possibilities through improvisation, the crowd responded with excitement. The crowd's energy encouraged them to explore and find the potential in their sound. They played in ways they hadn't in earlier shows and in ways they couldn't in their jam sessions at the house. The band felt like they could play all night long. The music didn't stop until the festival manager stepped onto the stage to end the set and introduce the next band.

The band packed up and headed back to Alcova. Their caravan arrived home, and they unloaded all of their equipment. Although it was late, they were wide awake and full of energy. No one wanted to go to bed yet, so they hung out in the kitchen to talk and eat. They all agreed that they'd played their best set yet. They had all felt something that they had never felt before. It was the rush of performing in an amphitheater venue and the exchange of energy to and from a large crowd of great fans. As they finished talking and eating, they left the kitchen to retire to their pads.

Davey stood alone for a minute in the kitchen and reflected on what he'd hoped to achieve. They had accomplished their goal of joining energy with the crowd. Together, they created a magical experience. Davey realized that while the band played, the crowd became more than just fans. In that moment, they became friends, and almost family. The crowd had become a part of The Bed Heads. Davey knew that performing live at festivals was what they were meant to do.

8

HIBERNATING BEAR

"Time Has Come Today"
— The Chambers Brothers

The days rode on and before they knew it, the semester was flying by. The band members poured their energy into teaching at the college and jamming each evening at the house. Word of The Bed Heads had spread across the central part of Wyoming. They had a standing show at Frontier Brewery every Saturday night, but touring was over for the season.

Early one Saturday morning in mid-November, Stella enjoyed her usual cup of coffee on the front porch. She watched the squirrels scamper as they prepared for winter. She found herself lost in the songs of the various birds as their melodies filled the crisp fall air. She was thinking of the weeks to come when it dawned on her that every one of the band members worked at the college. And they all have their summers free. What if they got serious about touring festivals next summer?

About that time, Davey walked onto the porch and Stella told him about her epiphany. Davey's wheels rolled with possibilities. They went inside and asked the rest of the band to join them in the kitchen. Stella shared her idea with everyone and they quickly agreed to tour.

"As much as I love jamming at home and playing shows at Frontier, those don't have the same feel as playing that festival," said Stella.

"I agree," said Maggie, "the energy at the festival was magical. I can't wait to play more of them."

"Right on, the festival crowd felt different, like a community or something. Like their role was as important as ours," said Joey.

Rubin said, "The audience communicated to us without words, you know?"

"Yeah, the crowd felt like family, like they were part of The Bed Heads," added Davey.

"I hope we can capture that magic again," Maggie said.

"Oh, we will," Rubin said.

With all of this talk about playing live, the band decided that they needed to jam. So, they headed into the parlor to start the fun.

Throughout the winter, Davey worked to develop a tour schedule for the band. He had traveled all over Wyoming to attend festivals of one kind or another for over nineteen years. He knew the festivals would make excellent venues, and he knew that Wyomingites loved music and loved to hear it live. Because he was such a friendly guy, he had made lots of friends and acquaintances throughout the years. He reached out to people he had met in his travels while he planned the tour to find out which festivals were happening next year.

Before long, he had organized a full touring schedule. He asked Bear to review it one day at the college. Davey looked at the schedule, made a couple of the changes Bear suggested, and then decided that it was doable. Now, he just needed to share it with the band.

After breakfast on Saturday morning, Davey asked for the band's attention. "Everybody, I have an announcement to make... we have a tour schedule!"

"What?" the group said as a whole.

"I've worked it out," Davey said. "It's just like we discussed after our first festival. We love to play together. We have a solid connection with the audience that we can only experience at festivals. We have a great sound, and we all have the summer off."

Now this was a big step facing the band. Even though they had talked about it before, the memory of that conversation had faded somewhat. They did love to jam and do gigs together, but touring was a whole new proposition. Seeing the schedule made touring seem shockingly real.

"How on earth will we be able to do all of this?" Maggie asked.

"We'll camp out," said Davey.

"Camp out? We need a plan," said Maggie emphatically with a hint of anxiety in her voice. "It currently takes three vehicles to get us and our equipment to a single festival. What will we eat? Also, I don't do well with nature."

"Maggie, nature is all around us," said Joey.

"Let's do it!" said Rubin, always a free spirit. "We can live off the land."

"Look," Davey said, "it will be fun. When my kids were little, we began to camp out and go on these wonderful adventures! In fact, my wife and I used to tell our girls stories along the way to pass the time and entertain each other. It was such a time of peace and tranquility. Can you think of a better way to spend our summer? And I'm sure we'll make some sensational memories of our own along the way that—"

"Maggie has a great point," said Stella, gently interrupting Davey. "We need to think about reliable transportation. We need to plan our route to decrease travel time. There are several other items we need to think through. Basically, like she said, we need a plan."

"Absolutely. I've already included some of that in our tour schedule," said Davey as he unrolled a large map of Wyoming on the kitchen table. "You see here," pointing to the circles around festival locations, "there are camp grounds located around several of the towns where we will be playing."

Davey stepped back from the map to give the others a chance to look. "I thought we could work together to finish the details of our travel plan, or rather, our travel adventures."

"Exactly!" said Joey. "I'm in."

"It sounds like you have really thought about this, Wavey Davey," said Maggie. "I'm down with planning our travel adventures."

"Oh yeah, I was thinking we could visit all of these famous state and national parks along the way," Davey said, pointing to the map.

"Sounds like this could be both entertaining and educational," said Stella.

"Great!" said Rubin. "I can't wait! Only one question... how will we get to these places? I don't know about you, but taking all of our vehicles from place to place will be a drag."

"Well," said Joey, "we should find a groovy bus or something like that. That's what all of the bands use these days."

"Great idea!" said Stella. "Now all we have to do is find a bus. A vintage bus would be so cool!"

"Well," said Davey, "it's funny that you mention it, I actually—" He was interrupted by a knock at the front door. "That's probably my friend from the engineering department. He is super smart." He got up from the table and started walking out of the kitchen. "He knows about the latest gadgets and even helped me with the logistics for our tour."

The band members looked at each other in a state of confusion. This was the first time Davey had mentioned anything to them about a friend coming over.

"I guess we should follow you?" Maggie asked.

With that, the group got up to follow Davey on his way to the front door. "What's this guy's name?" asked Rubin.

Davey paused and turned back towards his followers. "It's Bear, you know the guy from the engineering department that modified our wall phone. He is so connected to the world and new technology. His name is Stanley, but everyone calls him, 'Bear,' because he's hard to find, like a hibernating bear. Sometimes he's gone for periods of time, but he always comes back."

Davey paused for a moment, then added, "By the way, I invited him to come over because I wanted you all to meet him." He turned back around and started walking towards the front door again.

"That would make sense as to why he is currently knocking on our door," Joey said sarcastically.

Davey opened the door and a slender red-headed young man was standing there. He looked as if he couldn't be more than 20 years old. He was easily over six feet tall and rather thin. This combination made him look even taller than he actually was.

"Hello, Bear," Davey said in a welcoming and friendly voice.

Bear stood in the doorway, his eyes scanning the curious faces until settling on the one he thought he knew. He wanted to take out his journal to check his notes, but decided he had better not. Could that be a young Professor Hart? From his research, he knew Maggie had blond hair. Bear saw that Maggie was standing next to Davey, which meant Stella was behind her. Joey was definitely the one grinning. He expected meeting everyone to be exciting, but he didn't realize how starstruck he'd feel. He had goosebumps. Davey invited Bear in and introduced him to each member of the band.

"You're just in time. I was talking to the band about an old bus sitting in my barn," said Davey. "I'm not sure this is the bus everyone had in mind. Does anybody want to see it?"

"Yeah, I would love to see it," Rubin said.

"Far out! You have a bus?" exclaimed Stella. "I have got to see this."

They all headed towards the kitchen and out the back door towards the barn. They were so excited to see this mysterious bus that they didn't even bother to put on coats. Davey led them through the snow about 100 yards from the house to a barn with faded chestnut brown siding and a silver corrugated tin roof.

Davey said, "Okay guys, this isn't much, but maybe it will do."

9

MYSTERIOUS ODORS

"With a Little Help from My Friends"
— Joe Cocker

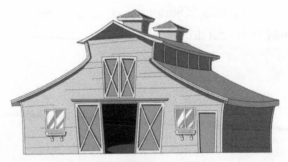

With anticipation, the barn doors slowly creaked opened. As the sunlight reflected off the snow and cast light a few feet into the barn, they began to see the outline of a large metal object. Little by little, the front of a GMC PD-4501 Scenicruiser bus came into view. The details were still cloaked in the darkness of the barn.

"Come on, guys, let's get out of the cold," said Stella.

Rubin took a few steps into the barn, but then stopped in awe. He stood there, gazing at the enormous metal work of art while the others filed past. Bear stopped next to Rubin and saw the look of admiration on his face. At that moment, he knew he had found a kindred spirit in young Rubin. He studied Rubin's face for a moment, looking for the Professor Hart he had met previously. He realized quickly that Professor Hart's youthful exuberance had faded little over the years. He leaned over and commented to Rubin in a low voice, "It's beautiful, isn't it? There's a lot of potential here."

Rubin glanced at Bear and said, "Yeah, I'm digging it. We can do a lot with this bus. It's a beautiful machine, man. I love it!"

Bear replied, "This bus will travel to so many cool places and take the band on so many awesome adventures. You guys might not be able to imagine it yet, but trust me, it will."

"Have you been on this bus before?" asked Stella.

"Well, not at this date in time," answered Bear.

"Far out, man! You're a visionary, just like me," said Rubin.

"Yeah, I can see how important this bus is to your dream," replied Bear.

Davey finished rolling back and securing the barn doors when Stella asked, "Wavey Davey, can we see more? Does this barn have a light?"

"Absolutely," said Davey as he walked to the side and flipped a switch. The band stepped farther into the barn to get a full look at the bus. As the halogen lights warmed up, they gradually illuminated the bus and its true condition.

Measuring 40 feet from bumper to bumper, it was longer than the average bus. In fact, it was the longest bus any of them had ever seen. The top of the bus was different too. While most buses were the same height from front to back, this one rose even higher after the first 10 feet, giving the impression that it had either an additional level or a really tall ceiling. The exterior was a murky silver with a dull blue stripe under the windows, most of which were cracked, missing, or askew. Some, if not all, of the tires on the left side were flat, making the entire bus look slightly lopsided.

Maggie and Joey exchanged glances. Davey noticed their concern and acknowledged, "Like I said, it's a bus but maybe not what you were looking for."

Stella replied, "I think it has great potential. The shape is interesting. It reminds me of the Humphead Maori Wrasse."

Maggie looked at Stella. "A what?"

Stella replied, "Yeah, it's a long fish with a big forehead."

"This will be a great project!" Rubin exclaimed as he ran his hands along the metal skin of the bus. "We can start on it now and have it done by the end of the semester."

"It's the beginning of February and the semester ends the last week of May. That gives us a little over four months to complete the project. Is that enough time?" asked Maggie.

Davey explained, "You're right, it will need a lot of work. I imagine it has been here close to 10 years. I was storing it for a friend, but when he moved to California, he decided to leave it with me. I wondered what I would do with it. I'd sort of forgotten it was here. So, what do you think?"

"Wow, it's a blank canvas! We can put a cool psychedelic paint job on this and make it look really groovy. This is going to be OUR tour bus!" said Joey.

"I love this bus," Stella said, "and I believe we have the ability to make it into anything we want it to be. But I'm just noticing how cold it is in here and we have three more months of winter. In Wyoming. We need to find a way to heat this barn so we can actually work on our project."

Davey said, "Well, it looks like this will be the first step in our project planning. Who wants to be on the barn heating committee?"

Rubin's hand shot up in the air. "I'd be down with trying to figure that out."

"Okay, so we have roughly four months to go. When do we have our first concert?" asked Maggie.

"Based on Wavey Davey's map, this project would need to be done by late May," commented Stella. "Our first festival is on Decoration Day in Buffalo."

"That's plenty of time," said Joey.

"I can't stand here any longer! I need to see this whole bus," Stella said.

"Yeah, let's check out the other side," said Joey.

The band began walking towards the back of the bus. Stella was the first to disappear around the rear bumper as she moved to the other side. Bear pointed out the storage compartment doors to Rubin as they walked by. Maggie was pleased about the surprisingly good condition of the back window. Joey picked at the corner of a sticker that had started peeling off the bumper. Davey slowly walked behind everyone else, surveying to himself how well the bus had held up over its decade in storage. At their own pace, everyone circled around the perimeter of the bus, subconsciously gravitating back toward its door.

Stella stepped closer to the door of the bus, trying to peer into the window. A film covered the glass and made it difficult to see inside. She turned to Davey and said, "I can't wait to see the inside! Can we please go in?"

"Yeah, I'd feel more comfortable about its potential if I could see the rest of it," added Maggie.

"Of course," Davey replied. He reached past Stella for the door handle. After a couple of swift tugs, the door loosened. Davey slid his fingers into the gap between the door and the frame of the bus, pulling hard on the door's edge. When the door opened, the pneumatic switch activated the air valve for the front suspension. As the air in the suspension released, the bus began to lower.

"Well, at least that's one thing we don't have to fix," said Rubin.

With the door finally open, Stella rushed excitedly past Davey and ran up the steps. One by one, they all followed Stella into the bus.

Once everyone was inside, they exchanged glances and looked around to figure out the types and sources of the variety of smells filling the air. Maggie was the first to comment about the mysterious aroma. "Well, it definitely has a unique odor. Or odors," she said, "that we might need to address in our project plan. Perhaps that should be next on the list after heating the barn."

Joey reached out and gently put his hand on Maggie's shoulder. "Maggie, I've got a feeling you're the right person for that job."

Bear added, "Don't worry Maggie, you'll get rid of the smell. Trust me."

"It's really dusty and that musty smell is usually a combination of water and dust. Sitting here it will get dusty, of course, and as you know, broken windows won't keep out moisture," said Davey.

Rubin looked up at the ceiling, pointed to the light penetrating through several of the rusted rivets, and added, "It's also likely coming through there. I need to find a ladder to get a better look at the outside. We may have to replace some or all of the roof."

"Back to the smell issue. It might also come from there," Maggie said, pointing to the bathroom door near the base of the steps leading to the upper level.

"It has a bathroom! And it has beds on the upper level! Guys, this isn't just a bus. It's a motorhome. Somebody's put a lot of work converting this to a home on wheels!" said

Stella. "Wavey Davey, what's the story of this bus?"

Davey explained that his friend had purchased the bus from the city and converted it to a motorhome. Davey's friend and his family used the bus to travel across the country. He explained how the luggage racks were removed and replaced with cabinets. They had replaced the seats on the lower level with padded benches that ran along either side of the bus. Underneath the padding on each bench, there was an access door for a storage compartment. Davey's friend wanted to maximize the utilization of space to keep his family comfortable and equipped for cross country travel.

"I love the natural light. Imagine going down the road with the sunshine flowing through these windows and skylights. Man, think about this though. At night we can look up and see the moon and the stars," said Joey.

Rubin interjected with a smile, "Unfortunately if we don't get that roof fixed, we will be seeing more of the sun, moon, and stars than you want. Especially when it rains."

Joey chuckled as he gently patted Rubin on the back, "You're going to fix that roof. And I'm going to paint a mural in here. Probably, well, maybe on the ceiling? Or possibly on the wall. I don't know yet."

"With all of this natural light, I wonder if we could build in a little herb garden? We could grow mint to put in our tea," Stella suggested.

Bear sat in the driver's seat, staring intently at the control panel. He knew he had to show that he was loyal, honest, and capable of contributing to the band. If the band members got a good vibe from him, he would be in a better position to help guide their destiny. After careful consideration, he turned to Rubin and said, "It'd be really cool to wire this bus for sound. You guys could tune your instruments on the road before the show. And maybe add speakers throughout the bus."

"I dig it! We could wire it for speakers on the outside too," said Rubin.

"Yes, we could," agreed Bear, thankful that Rubin seemed to appreciate the idea.

"That's it! We need to plan how we're going to transform this motorhome into our touring bus. There's enough storage for all of our equipment. We can make this all one level. And, there's bedding for five. We can expand that for six," said Davey.

"Six? There's only five of us," said Maggie.

"We might want to bring other friends on our adventures," replied Davey. "Like Bear. We could really use a sound guy."

"I liked Bear's suggestion of tuning our instruments on the road. That would be helpful," said Stella.

"What do you think about adding him to our group?" Davey asked.

"Sounds good, but let's talk more about it," Maggie said.

"I agree. As much as I love this bus, I'm freezing out here. Could we talk about this back at the house?" asked Stella.

They exited the bus, closed the barn doors, and headed towards the house. During the walk back, the group talked over the possibility of fixing up the bus. The ideas were flowing. Once they got to the kitchen, Davey put on a fresh pot of coffee and a kettle for tea while the others sat down at the table. Everyone agreed that the motorhome would make a great touring bus for the band. They joked about how their new tour bus would be as unique as their sound and individual personalities.

When the kettle whistled and the coffee was ready, everyone headed to the counter to pick out a mug and fill it with their favorite hot beverage. Bear's eyes fell on the orange jar next to the coffee pot. "Wait, is that Tang?" he asked excitedly.

"It sure is. Where are our manners? Would you like a drink, Bear?" asked Maggie.

Bear replied, "If you don't mind, I'll stir up some Tang for myself."

Maggie handed him a glass as the focus of the group's conversation returned to their project. They decided that Joey could paint the inside with a ginormous mural to reflect their travels. Maggie could start the planning process. Stella could work on the floor plan. Rubin and Davey could figure out which parts were salvageable and what they would actually need to replace in order for the bus to run.

When Rubin mentioned the wiring they'd need for speakers, Bear said, "The other thing we could do is put in connections so you guys could plug in your instruments on the outside of the bus."

"You're in!" said Rubin.

It was settled. Everyone agreed and The Bed Heads had a tech guy. Bear sighed with relief. Now they could get started on the bus.

SOMETHING NEW

"Let's Work Together"
— Canned Heat

The next morning after they finished their breakfast, Maggie stood up and asked for everyone's attention. She held a clipboard with a sheet of paper containing role assignments for the bus restoration project. She opened her mouth to read from her list when the doorbell rang. Maggie said, "Oh, I'll be right back." She walked out of the kitchen and a moment later, returned with Bear.

"Bear!" Rubin and Davey said simultaneously.

"As you can see, I invited Bear over this morning so I can give everyone their assigned roles," Maggie said.

Davey got up from the table. "Good morning, Bear. Have you eaten? Did you have breakfast already? Can I can make you some eggs? Make you some toast? Coffee? Tea?"

Joey said with a smile, "Maybe some Tang?"

"As a matter of fact, I would love some Tang!" said Bear. Tang reminded him of growing up with the space program. The ability to experience retro things before they considered them retro was one of his favorite aspects of time travel. For instance, he found telephone tables and rotary phones to be extremely interesting. Nobody used either of those anymore, but he enjoyed sitting at the table by Davey's front door and messing with the rotary dial. He liked the feeling of poking his finger into the hole by the nine, rotating the wheel all the way to the finger stop, and listening to the clicking sound as it returned to its original position.

Maggie began again, "While Bear is making some Tang, I'd like to share more about your roles and the different project teams."

Maggie assigned Stella, Davey, and herself to The Walk-Through Checklist Development Team. She assigned Davey and Rubin to The

Motor and Other Parts Team. Joey, Stella, and Bear were on The Interior Design Team. She told them that Bear and Davey were assigned to The Electrical and Technology Team. After discussing the purpose for each team and each team member's role, she distributed the schedule. "I will meet with each team to get a list of the things that need to be replaced, rebuilt, or remodeled."

The group sat quietly for a moment, shifting slightly in their seats. Joey raised his hand, "Um, I have a—"

Maggie quickly added, "I can explain more when we meet. The first team is going to the barn in 35 minutes, so we need to get ready. I'll meet you there. Thank you, everyone." She turned and left the kitchen.

Joey said, "I don't know about you guys, but I'm grabbing my coat and heading out there now."

"Right behind you, man," said Rubin.

Within seven minutes, everyone had changed into their winter gear and were greeted by Maggie as they entered the barn. Rubin said, "Hey Maggie, I appreciate all the effort you put into this, but before we do anything, we've got to make this place warmer."

"Rubin, I believe you were leading that committee. Does anyone want to volunteer to help him?" Stella asked.

Bear raised his hand.

"Groovy. While they're making this environment more comfortable to work in, the rest of us can examine the outside and the inside of the bus to, like Maggie said earlier in the kitchen, develop a list of what needs to be replaced, rebuilt, or remodeled," Stella said.

Davey agreed, "It sounds like a great plan. Let's get started. I suggest we walk around the bus to see what we need to do to get the bus stabilized. Once it's stable and safe, we can explore the body and drivetrain in more detail."

Davey fired up the air compressor so they could inflate the tires and put air into the air pneumatic system, which controlled the brakes, suspension, and doors. Rubin and Bear headed off to explore how they could better seal up the barn and generate some source of heat. Davey showed Joey how to hook up the air hose to the air pneumatic system and fill the reserve air tank so they could easily open and close the bus's door.

Davey handed Maggie and Stella tire blocks and asked them to wedge one behind each tire. He explained that he wanted to make sure that the bus wouldn't roll. Joey had finished filling the reserve tank. Maggie and Stella put the blocks behind each of the ten tires. Davey made sure the brake was set on the bus and began filling up the flat tires on the left side. After verifying with Davey that it was safe to go into the bus, Stella, Maggie, and Joey went in to inspect the interior.

After a few minutes, Joey climbed off the bus and found Davey, who was finishing his visual inspection of the bus's exterior. As a sculptor who had worked with and understood the nuances of different metals, Joey had concerns about the condition of the roof. He explained to Davey that the entire roof needed to be replaced. Joey and Davey finished making the checklist of the things to replace on the exterior, like the tires, three windows, and of course, the roof. Maggie finished the interior checklist and Stella finished a rough sketch of the new floor plan.

Rubin and Bear met up with Joey and Davey to talk about heating the barn. Stella and Maggie stepped off the bus after hearing their voices. Maggie smiled and asked, "How's it going with The Barn Heating Team?"

Rubin explained that they needed to get some lumber and insulation to close up gaps in the siding and keep the cold wind out. Bear informed everyone that they'd found an old coal-burning stove that they could modify to put out more heat. They'd need to go to the store and get supplies to convert it over to a gas burning stove and build a duct system to spread the heat throughout the barn. Joey and Davey told the group that the metal in the bus's roof was so deteriorated that the entire roof would have to be replaced.

Stella said, "It would be groovy if we could have a panoramic ceiling in the bus."

"Do you mean like a dining car on a train?" asked Bear.

"Do you know what would be perfect? We could go to the scrap metal place and get one of the domes off an old rail car," Joey said.

Stella and Maggie shared their ideas for the bus's new floor plan with the group. "We thought we could add a little kitchen, another bathroom, and couches for seating. With the rail car top, we can have that awesome view," said Stella.

They took turns looking at the floor plan and Stella encouraged them to add their ideas to the diagram. Once everyone agreed on the final design, Joey and Davey headed to the scrapyard to look for parts. Rubin and Bear headed to the hardware store to pick up supplies. Maggie and Stella retired to the kitchen to look at the Sears catalog for small appliances, fixtures, and fabrics.

Over the next two months, they made significant progress. The work was long and hard. Sometimes the group wanted to give up. There was a lot of trial, error, and differences of opinion. Thankfully, Rubin and Bear not only solved the barn's heating problem, they created a comfortable environment. Joey and Davey had removed the roof and installed the new panoramic rail top.

Joey was enthusiastic about getting started on the interior mural but the dust kicked up from the other projects made it difficult. Timing was a struggle. He started and stopped twice before deciding that the mural would need to be one of the final steps in the restoration process. Stella helped negotiate the timeline for everyone while gathering the appliances, fixtures, and fabrics needed for the interior. She began using the back of the barn to store everything until it was time to be installed. Joey sketched the design on the bus's metal skin to prepare for painting.

Davey replaced all the tires and brake shoes. As he was installing the new brake lines under the bus, Maggie and Bear were plumbing the bathroom. Several times as Davey was securing the brake line to the frame of the bus, a saw blade came through the floor. The first time the blade barely broke the surface. The last time it was just inches from his head. He wisely decided to wait to finish the brakes until the plumbing was completed.

Maggie fixed the smell issue radiating from the front bathroom. Davey and Joey helped Maggie fabricate the rear bathroom. Removing the engine and transmission was more difficult than anticipated. After a few failed attempts, Rubin fashioned a cradle to lift them with a front loader. He needed the help of Davey, Bear, and Joey to negotiate the space, so Maggie offered to drive the front loader. It took her a few tries to get the hang of operating the controls. Once they were removed and relocated, Rubin started the process of rebuilding. Bear rewired the bus and installed the driver's compartment.

By the end of the two months, the band was growing tired of the long days and the hard work. During a lunch break one Saturday, they started talking about how they've been spending so much time on the bus that they didn't have much time to practice and jam together. They were becoming frustrated with themselves and with each other as the project lingered on. As they ate and talked, they discussed how they were becoming disconnected from each other and that they missed their jam sessions. Davey brought up the point that their jam sessions weren't just about learning the songs; it was about learning to connect through improvisation and learning how to recognize and build on the strengths of each musician. Davey reminded the group that every time they jammed, it wasn't about achieving perfection, it was about creating something new.

Inspired by the moment, Joey said, "Everybody, grab your instruments! We need to jam." And so, they jammed.

11

BEADED CURTAIN

"Built to Last"
— Grateful Dead

Over the final two months of the bus restoration process, the band broke up the work by building jam sessions into their schedule. Working hard to create something new, everyone felt more connected to each other and time passed more pleasantly.

With two weeks to go, the team hurried to apply the finishing touches to the bus. Joey stayed up late, painting the final coat on the exterior and adding more detail to the interior mural. Stella and Maggie finished fitting out the sleeping quarters and hanging a beaded curtain to mark its entrance. Bear completed wiring the new internal sound system for the band to jam and tune on the road. He also put in new communications equipment and dashboard controls.

The bus restoration project was almost complete, just in time for their first festival of the summer. They were scheduled to leave the next morning. Everyone gathered to watch as Rubin and Davey carefully lowered the engine and transmission onto the motor mounts in the bus's engine bay. After hooking up the transmission and engine, Rubin said, "This bus is going to use a lot of fuel. Man, if only we could find a way to make this thing more efficient."

"I don't know how to make it more efficient, but I do know how to use fewer fossil fuels," Stella said. "When Bear was installing the new fuel pump and fuel tank, I had him add a heating element to the fuel tank and fuel line."

"I understand why you have a block heater for a diesel, but why add a heating element in the fuel tank?" Rubin responded.

Stella told them about her idea for biodiesel and then showed them the biodiesel plant she had assembled in a back stall of the barn. She explained how she created biodiesel from used cooking oil. She reassured Rubin that they could use it to fuel the bus as long as there was a heater in the tank to keep it from coagulating.

Rubin and Stella discussed in more detail how biodiesel is made and how it works. After their talk, Rubin felt comfortable letting Stella put her biodiesel in the tank to test the engine. Rubin started the engine and let it run for a while and the engine sounded strong and smooth with the biodiesel. Soon, everyone noticed that the exhaust smelled like french fries.

Davey completed the final walk-through with Bear. He stepped onto the bus and was immediately in awe of the new interior. It was colorful and inviting. He thought the hardwood flooring was a durable choice. Davey sat in the crushed blue velvet driver's seat and looked at the dashboard and the communication panel that Bear added. He liked the new cup holder and the armrests. Davey looked at the dashboard, noticing the circular fuel gauge and speedometer. "Wait, that's not a cathode ray tube display," he said with a hint of confusion in his voice.

"No, it's LED. Uh, new technology currently being developed for the consumer market," Bear replied. It was true though. LED would soon be used in calculators. Albeit, expensive calculators. He wondered if he was pushing his luck with introducing this much futuristic technology.

On the side panel, there were several new buttons, switches, and dials. Only a few of them were labeled. Bear said not to worry about the others right now. He explained that the "COMM" button enabled them to contact him when he's back on campus. The "INT sound" toggle switch controlled the internal plugins for the band's instruments and the overhead sound system. The "EXT sound" toggle switch controlled the external plugins and sound system for the band's instruments. The "AWN" dial allowed them to extend the outside awning.

Bear explained that when the engine was off, they had to turn the generator on or the appliances and lights would drain the battery. He further added that to start the generator, turn the "GEN" toggle switch to ON and press the green "START" button.

Behind either side of the driver's seat were long, u-shaped couches against each wall. Davey lifted one of the brown and psychedelic paisley cushions to check the latches on the under-seat storage bins. The couches could easily seat the entire band. There was a separate control panel for volume in the seating area behind the driver. The windows above the couches had geometric mod patterned curtains.

Davey walked down the aisle between the two couches to the dining area. They had removed the original bathroom and added a small kitchen with a sink, stove, refrigerator, and overhead cabinets. He was relieved that they'd found a way to secure the coffee maker to the counter. He opened and closed the oven door to take a quick look inside.

There was an eating area with two booths they were lucky to buy from G-Ma's Diner during their remodel. Davey sat in a booth and looked up at the celestial mural that Joey had painted on the ceiling. The cosmic mural was a swirl of blues and purples with silver stars and a big yellow and orange sun. Davey couldn't help but be impressed with Joey's talent. Staring at the various shades of blue and purple, he was mesmerized by the depth Joey had created in the mural's background. He thought he could spot Orion.

Behind the second booth was a staircase leading to the new exterior door they had installed. Across from the new door was a simple bathroom with a toilet and a tiny sink. Davey opened the bathroom door and noticed that it smelled fresh and clean. He stepped inside, closed the door, and tested the facilities. After washing his hands, Davey left the bathroom and headed to his right.

Hanging in the doorway dividing the living area from the sleeping quarters was a brightly colored beaded curtain. Davey walked through the curtain and smiled at the sound they made as he passed. He was pleased that they had decided on replacing the old roof with the dome of an observation car.

The new roof gave them enough space to add three bunks with affixed ladders on either side of the hallway. The top bunk was right at the level of the observation dome, and Davey could only imagine what the view would be like up there at night. Each of the bunks had their own storage, a bar to hang up clothes, and a privacy curtain. They had tie-dyed their own curtains, so each was unique in color and design. The curtains were fun to make and enabled them to personalize their bunks.

Davey rolled himself onto the lowest bunk to test the mattress and see how close his feet were to the storage area. Davey stretched out on his back with his hands behind this head. "Ahh, perfect! This is comfortable, and I have plenty of room. I'll take this one."

With a wink, Bear switched the tie-dyed curtains to put Davey's at that bunk. Davey reluctantly rolled out of his new bunk, thankful that the beds were so comfortable. At the end of the hallway, there was a full-sized bathroom. Since the bathroom stretched across the entire width of the bus, they had enough room to include a bathtub as well as a toilet and sink. He finished his walk-through, and he and Bear exited the bus through the new side door.

Seeing the entire band waiting for him, Davey announced, "This is the most awe-inspiring tour bus in the existence of tour buses! We did an awesome job!"

Stella excitedly asked, "Did you notice The Destroilet I installed in the rear bathroom?"

"Destroy what?" Davey asked.

"It's a Destroilet! It's an incinerating toilet. It literally incinerates human waste," explained Stella.

"A toilet can do that? Outta site!" Rubin said.

"On that note, let's jam!" said Joey.

After the jam session, everybody loaded their instruments on the bus and went back to the house. They munched on cold cuts and talked for a while. After about an hour, Davey retired to the library while the others continued to their rooms.

Davey sat in the library, relaxing and thinking in his favorite green recliner. He opened his tin from Donells Candies and selected the perfect Dark Chocolate Pecan Cluster. The semester was over, the bus was finished, and the summer tour was about to begin. He marveled at how much his life had changed since his last summer break. He missed his wife and thought about how much she would have enjoyed their tour bus. He knew that she would have loved riding in it with him and their girls. But he knew he couldn't have done all of that work on his own. And if he had, the bus wouldn't have quite the same personality without the contributions of the band. He was thankful that they had come into his life. He'd promised his wife he would try to bring back the music, and he knew she'd be happy that he had. He felt it in his soul that she was proud of him, and that gave him a sense of peace. He was ready to keep truckin' on.

INTERLUDE

"Not Fade Away"
— Buddy Holly

Stanley paced outside of the alumni center on campus. In between his travels, he had monitored the changes in the exhibit to see how their timeline had been progressing. The most important change was coming. Or not, depending on the band.

All he had to do was walk inside and look at the 1960s display. He gave The Bed Heads what they needed to fix the single variable that stood between them and their dream. He'd set the stage, even getting them to live together at Wavey Davey's house. Although, he admitted, that part wasn't completely intentional. His suggestion had worked far better than he'd intended.

For their first outing with the bus, he would deliberately be absent. He knew he could not interfere with the space-time continuum any further. They needed to fix the bus on their own in order to alter their own paths.

He kept pacing for forty-two more minutes, until finally, he opened the door and stepped inside.

12

TRUCKIN' UP TO BUFFALO

"Midnight Special"
— Lead Belly

It was 7:37 a.m. Even though the first gig of their tour was only about two hours away, the group wanted to get an early start. Davey sat in the driver's seat with a fresh thermos of coffee in his cup holder. He turned to the other band members and said, "Here it goes," as he fired up the engine. Davey released the parking brake and eased the bus out of the barn. The bus rolled down the lane and then turned east onto Highway 220. As they passed through Casper, Maggie was excited that the bus gave her a better view of all the prairie dogs standing near their holes in the meadow at the corner of Collins Drive and Poplar Street. She asked Davey to pause a little longer at the intersection before they continued up the road to merge onto US 25 North.

They were going up the country as they cruised along the highway. They settled in and got comfortable. Joey and Rubin went straight to their bunks and crashed. Maggie and Stella lounged on the couches behind Davey.

"Hey, Joey?" Rubin said as he stretched out in his bunk. "Man, just think, one year ago we hardly even knew each other. But since then, we formed a band, we built this awesome bus, we've eaten SPAM together, and now we are on our first official road trip."

Joey did not reply.

"Hey man, you still down there?" Rubin leaned over to look at the bunk below him. "Joey?"

The long nights over the past few weeks and the rhythm of the highway had lulled Joey to sleep. Rubin rolled back into his bunk and watched the clouds suspended in the big blue sky. Before he knew it, he was fast asleep.

An hour later, they were almost halfway there. They were making their way past the little town of Kaycee when the bus jerked and sputtered. Davey was able to nurse the bus to the shoulder of the highway before the engine completely died. Davey set the parking brake and turned the ignition off. He had to get in contact with Bear for assistance.

Bear had told them to press the "COMM" button and, after hearing the tone, it would connect them with his office back in the engineering department. From there, he could run diagnostics on the bus or help with any problem that might arise. He had to stay on campus for the summer, so it just made sense.

Davey pushed the button labeled, "COMM," and said, "Bear, do you copy? We seem to have a problem with the bus."

Davey waited. Bear did not reply.

"Bear, I repeat, we are having a problem with the bus. Can you please run diagnostics and tell us what's wrong?" Davey prompted.

There was no response.

Davey said, "Well guys, it looks like we have lost communication with Bear. We're on our own to figure out what's wrong with this bus."

Stella chimed in, "Do you think it has anything to do with the fuel?"

"Possibly," Davey said. "All we know right now is that the tank is almost full. Rubin and I will have to open the engine bay and troubleshoot the problem."

By this time, Rubin had woken up and come to the front of the bus. "What's happening, Wavey Davey?"

Davey explained how the bus had stopped working and that he was unable to communicate with Bear. Everyone but Joey disembarked and started to investigate. Davey and Rubin opened the engine bay cover and examined the engine and components. They found everything in working order and could not see any leaks. Davey went back on the bus and tried to start it again with no success. He turned the ignition off and returned to the others at the back of the bus. Rubin indicated that the engine was turning over, but it sounded like it was not getting any fuel.

Just then Maggie remembered hearing Bear say something about bringing an extra fuel filter. "We should probably check the fuel filter. I remember Bear telling us to bring a spare."

They checked and sure enough, it was clogged!

"That's right," Stella said. "I forgot about that. It's one of the things I learned when studying biodiesel. When you first use biodiesel, the fuel filter will have to be changed a couple of times. At least until the wax from the petroleum works its way out of the system."

"Aww, man," Rubin said, "the fuel lines. We did not replace them during the restoration. There must have been enough diesel left in the line to cause wax to form in the fuel filter. I did pick up an extra filter before we left, like Bear suggested, but I can't find it so it is probably sitting on the workbench back in the barn."

"Well, let's hope the Sinclair station in the friendly town of Kaycee has one for sale," said Maggie. "Who's walking?"

About that time, Joey stepped off the bus and headed towards them.

"Come on, we're taking a walk back to the Sinclair station to hopefully buy a new fuel filter," Rubin informed Joey.

"Well then, let's do this," Joey said. They waved to the others and started walking the mile and a half back to Kaycee. "Do we even know if they have a fuel filter?"

"Nope, but we're going to find out if they do. What a trip we've been on this year. Started to tell you about this on the bus, but you were in a solid state of unconsciousness," Rubin teased Joey.

"What, no man! I was just resting my eyes and contemplating the meaning of life and all," Joey said in a joking tone.

"That was some serious contemplation. Anyway, I was talking about the groovy things we've done since we all moved in together. I mean, we started a band and rebuilt this bus!"

"Yeah, and apparently we are still rebuilding it."

"Don't sweat it, bro. We're just working out all the bugs."

"That's one big bug, man. Let's hope our luck will carry us through and there will be a nice, beautiful fuel filter waiting for us in Kaycee."

"Yeah man, keep putting out those positive vibes. It will be there when we get there, my friend," Rubin said.

"It's true what you were rappin' about regarding the past year, you know, the band and all. It is really remarkable that a random group of people could respond to the same ad, form a band, and rebuild a bus that had been in a barn for 10 years."

"Yeah, bro. That mural you painted was incredible. And the outside of the bus? Wow, you blew me away with that."

"Thanks, man. I mean, you brought the life back to this bus. You rebuilt that engine and got it running. I mean, it doesn't run now, but it will."

"This is really more than a bus. I have a good feeling about where this bus is going to take us."

"I hope the bus is not like our music. I mean, I hope we're not always working on it," added Joey.

"Me too. I hope the bus and the band travel together for years."

"Definitely! I dig these road trips."

"Hey, there's the station!" Rubin said, pointing to the sign in the distance.

"Groovy! Maybe we can pick up snacks while we're there," said Joey.

Meanwhile, back at the bus, Davey started the generator to provide electrical power for the appliances. Maggie, Stella, and Davey boarded the bus and sat down in the booths. Davey made coffee while they waited for Rubin and Joey to return.

"You know," Maggie commented as they drank their coffee, "we're broken down by the side of the road, but just look around. It's beautiful!"

"Yeah," Davey said. "My family and I loved to travel and camp. There is just something about being in nature that cleanses the soul."

"This trip will be wondrous!" said Stella.

"Did I ever tell you about The Feathertons?" Davey asked. "One time, I was traveling with my family through the Wind River Canyon on our way to Yellowstone. All of a sudden, our engine quit as we heard a loud noise from the rear of the VW. Luckily, I was able to pull over to the side of the road and set the parking brake."

"Wow, that sounds similar to what happened today!" said Stella.

"Maybe that's why The Feathertons popped into my mind," said Davey.

"What happened next?" asked Maggie.

"Well, I checked the engine and found that the main belt had broken. Fortunately, I had a spare in the toolbox, but I knew it would take at least an hour to put the new one on. That's when I remembered the picture of a little family of birds that my daughter had brought home from school. I told a story to the kids as I worked on the bus to help pass time and keep them occupied. I named the bird family, The Feathertons," said Davey.

"Quick thinking with the story," said Maggie.

"The Feathertons! That's an adorable name for a bird family. How many birds had she drawn?" asked Stella.

"She drew six colorful birds, one for each of us," answered Davey. "After that first adventure, we told Featherton stories on roads trips and at bedtime. We sure had a lot of silly stories throughout the years. We came across so many learning opportunities on our adventures, and it was fun to work those into our stories. Mostly, The Feathertons were a chance for us to bond and enjoy each other's company."

"That sounds like fun," Stella said. "I'll bet those road trips were fab adventures."

Back on the road, Rubin and Joey were on their return trip from the Sinclair station. Rubin used the bottle opener on his keychain to pop the caps from the glass bottles of Goody Yellow Pop. He handed a bottle to Joey, put the bottle opener back in his pocket, and took a sip of the cold soda.

"The thing I love about music is the ability to have a new experience every time you play," Joey said.

"Yeah man, you can't be afraid to take risks," Rubin said.

"Absolutely! I mean, sometimes you have to let it ride. To give the music space to build and expand."

"It has to breathe. If the crowd's not in it, then the music isn't worth playing."

"Yeah, the greater the risk, the greater the reward," agreed Joey, taking a long drink.

"Somehow it always works itself out."

Davey, Maggie, and Stella stepped off the bus as Rubin and Joey came into view, each with empty bottles of Goody Yellow Pop. Joey held out a bag full of chocolate MoonPies, Clark Bars, Ho Hos, and Red Ropes licorice.

Rubin held up two fuel filters. "I know we only need one, but we bought a spare."

"We didn't want to have any more surprises. Bear will be proud," said Joey with a wink.

"Yeah, it's like the folks at Sinclair knew exactly what we needed," added Rubin.

Thirty minutes later, the crew was on their way again. "Good thing we left early," Stella said with a smile. "Buffalo, here we come!"

The group rolled into town around noon and drove to the venue. They cruised through the performer's parking lot and pulled into the spot where they saw the sign for "The Bed Heads." They had three hours before their concert. Davey and Stella left to hook up the water and electricity. Maggie and Rubin started preparing MacaroniOs and SpaghettiOs for lunch. Joey started bringing the guitars onto the bus so they could tune them.

Once Davey and Stella had returned, the group sat down in the booths to eat. After they finished eating, the band tried out the new internal sound system. Davey flipped the "INT sound" toggle switch to ON. Joey, the first to plug in, excitedly strummed his guitar, but there wasn't any sound coming from the internal speakers. They looked at each other, confused. Davey checked all the fuses. Right about that time, Rubin turned the dial on the wall labeled, "VOL," and said, "Try it again, Joey."

With that, Joey strummed again and the speakers came alive with sound. And it sounded good. As Davey and Stella plugged in and tuned their guitars, Rubin helped Maggie get her keyboard out of storage. He placed it on the table by the rear side door and plugged her keyboard into the sound system. The band talked about their setlist and picked out a few tunes to rehearse.

At 2:07 p.m., the talent manager knocked on the door to take them to the stage. The band brought out their instruments and opened the storage compartments to get the rest of their equipment. The talent manager's crew loaded the gear into their El Camino, and the band jumped into the talent manager's station wagon to head to the stage.

truckin' up to Buffalo

By 2:45 p.m., the band was set up, tuned, and ready to play. As they waited for their start time, the nerves heightened. It excited them to play, but they were a little anxious about how they would connect with this crowd. Would they be able to create the same experience with this audience that they had at their last festival?

"Introducing The Bed Heads!" a booming voice declared over thunderous applause. Joey turned to the band and said, "Make 'em swing!" as he launched into a rocking version of "All Along the Watchtower." The crowd responded to the band's energy. It surprised them how quickly the audience became energized and excited. Joey was ready to try something new. He wanted the crowd to get turned on and be carried away by the music. Joey decided to just let it rock.

During the second chorus, Joey nodded to Maggie and turned to make eye contact with Rubin as he rolled into a solo with the most honest spontaneity that the band had ever heard from him. From that point on, the song evolved into a leaderless cooperative featuring each of the members in a series of solos. It was like unassuming children playing catch on a pleasant Saturday afternoon. The direction of the music flowed from one band member to another.

As the band jammed, the crowd became more animated, dancing and twirling to the hypnotic sounds. Instead of playing their planned setlist of eleven songs, they could only finish five because they had expanded each song through improvisation. With the extended jam and solos, each song lasted at least ten minutes. The end of one song melted into the beginning of the next. The vibe from the crowd energized the band to continue exploring Joey's idea for something new.

They blinked, and it was over. This was one day they would never forget. This experience had shown them that the goal of every performance should be to try something new; not to replicate anything from the past. They would now let each performance be its own. Performances would become dynamic and flowing, alive with spontaneous energy from both the band and the crowd.

The trip back home to Alcova started with animated discussion.

"Did you see the girl with the four hula hoops? That was far out!" Joey said.

"Man, the food at these festivals rock!" Rubin said.

"Did you see people passing around little cups?" asked Joey.

"Yeah, I think they were sharing granola," said Stella.

"Too bad it didn't make it to the stage," Davey said.

"I wonder how granola would float in Jell-O salad," said Joey.

"Didn't you say, Wavey Davey, that you had Jell-O salad for a week?" Maggie said.

"We sure did. Meatloaf, corn, and mashed potatoes in Italian Salad Jell-O was the most interesting one my wife made. Cold, jiggly meatloaf. My family and I laughed about that for a while," Davey said.

"Did you top it with mayonnaise?" Rubin asked.

"Jell-O salad is art, man. You're not supposed to eat it!" Joey said.

Within 30 minutes, the energy had transitioned from excitement to a pleasant contentment. The adrenaline from the show had worn off and each of the band members went to different places in their minds and on the bus. Rubin and Stella retired to their bunks to listen to the rhythm of the road and watch the starry night sky. Joey and Maggie stretched out on the couches, listening to Count Basie playing softly through the overhead sound system.

Davey was feeling the effects of the long and exciting day. He repositioned himself in the crushed velvet driver's seat and opened his red plaid thermos to get some much-needed coffee. Unfortunately, the thermos was empty. Should he ask Rubin to make more? He decided to let him rest. How nice that would be, to nap on the ride back. To lounge on the couch or in his bunk. To be a passenger. Even with his family, he'd always been the one driving.

He had to stay focused. To keep truckin'. He had to keep the wheels turning and couldn't slow down, not even for coffee. With each mile he drove, he covered a little more ground.

He couldn't wait to talk to Bear tomorrow to figure out what had happened. He shifted in his seat, rolling his head from side to side to loosen his neck muscles. As they drove through

Casper, he felt a small burst of energy, knowing they were close to Alcova.

The wheels turned one last time as he parked the bus in the barn. He turned off the engine, set the parking brake, and said quietly to himself, "What a long strange trip it's been."

13

BUILT TO LAST

"The Music Never Stopped"
— Grateful Dead

The next morning after breakfast, Maggie and Joey unloaded the instruments. Stella worked on preparing another batch of biodiesel. Rubin changed the oil, cleaned out the fuel lines, and changed the fuel filter. Davey stopped by the barn. "I'm going to pick up Bear so we can solve the communication issue from yesterday. We'll get this fixed. I'll be back in an hour. I left a fresh pot of coffee for you at the house."

The band, never ones to resist coffee, took a break and returned to the kitchen. It wasn't long before they heard Davey's truck come up the driveway and continue towards the barn. They all headed outside to join Davey and Bear, who were pulling the barn doors open. The band noticed that the bed of Davey's truck was full of electronics and technology they had never seen before.

Maggie asked, "Wavey Davey, what's all of this stuff in the back of your truck?"

"I'm not sure exactly. Bear wanted to bring it over for the bus. We're going to unload it soon, but first I want him to look at the communication system," answered Davey while they secured the barn doors.

Bear walked into the barn and exclaimed, "Wow, I still can't get over how far out that bus looks! You really nailed it with that paint job, Joey."

"Yeah, it's a real psychedelic kaleidoscope of colors," said Joey.

"Hey, did you draw the mountains we see in the distance beyond Pathfinder Reservoir?" asked Stella.

"Yeah, I was inspired by the way the mountain peaks meet the sky," Joey replied.

"We only have five days, Bear! Five days!" reminded Davey. "We need to know what happened when the communications system failed. Let's go take a look."

They climbed onto the psychedelic bus. After a few minutes, Bear assured Davey, "I think we're close to figuring this out. We should create an alternate plan though, just in case another issue arises." Bear pointed to the "COMM" button on the dashboard and added, "So you said that you clicked this button here—"

"Yes, and nothing happened!" Davey interrupted.

"Okay, I think I see the problem," said Bear, already knowing the problem since he purposely did not respond to Davey that day. He felt bad ignoring him, but he knew it had been necessary. The Bed Heads needed to solve the problem themselves in order to protect the time bridge he secured in the space-time continuum.

He asked Davey to repeat the steps, but this time he took a small rectangle out of his pocket. The rectangle was black and had little buttons. As Davey pushed the button, Bear held the black rectangle up to his ear as though he was listening to something. "Yep, I'm getting nothing, but I know what it is."

Bear opened the side panel by the driver's seat, fished around in the compartment for a few seconds and said, "Aha! A loose wire. I think I fixed it."

They tested the system and it worked! Davey was relieved.

With that mystery solved, Bear told the group that he had brought over some new technology and asked for help unloading it into the barn. Bear spent the next few days installing and testing the new technology. Now that he knew their path was altering, he felt more comfortable contributing to the changes.

Meanwhile back at the house, the band continued with their preparations for the long road trip. Stella worked in the garden, getting everything planted. Davey and Rubin picked up supplies at Grant Street Grocery in Casper. Rubin was particularly excited about this cool tube of dehydrated potato chips he found, called "Pringle's Newfangled Potato Chips." Joey and Maggie worked on new songs.

One afternoon, Maggie walked into the parlor to see Joey pacing back and forth in front of the window. He appeared to be mouthing words.

"Hey, Joey," Maggie said, "going over a new tune?"

"Absolutely," said Joey, "I'm just trying to work out the chorus."

"Sing it to me and maybe I can help," Maggie said.

Joey told her that the song was called, "Soft Blue Dream." He explained how the first lyric talked about the sunlight shining through a stained-glass window, filling the room with a soft blue light during a certain time of day. The chorus is about a beautiful blond girl who loves to dance in that hazy blue light, and she's sad when it leaves. Eventually she realizes that even though it's gone today, it will be back tomorrow. Joey grabbed his guitar and Maggie sat at the piano. Together, they worked out the chorus and the musical arrangement to accompany the lyrics. They invited the rest of the band to join and develop their parts.

Over the next few days, they worked on that song and discussed the possibility of recording a demo. They decided instead to play it at their festival shows to see how the audience reacted. Stella suggested that they should try to record the song at the upcoming festival. That afternoon when Bear came into the house for lunch, they asked him about the possibility of recording their shows. Bear said that he'd do his best to get some type of recording equipment for this weekend and then try to get them something better for the rest of their tour. The band went back to practicing and jamming. They created loose setlists for their tour with the understanding that they'd continue to improvise each performance like they had at their last festival.

It was Thursday afternoon and finally time for Bear to reveal all the new technology he had installed on the bus. He asked the band to join him, motioning for them to sit on the couches. Bear pointed to the TV monitor he had mounted from the ceiling above the first booth in the kitchen. He explained that this was their new control center to help them plan their trips and provide navigational communication while on the road. He took the keyboard from its mount on the back of the first booth and showed how to plan their route from one festival to the next. The navigation system would give driving instructions to Davey through a speaker in the dashboard.

Bear had Davey turn on the ignition to the bus and press the "COMM" button. The group heard a ringing sound coming from Bear's back pocket. Bear pulled out the same black rectangle he had used that prior Sunday with Davey to test the communications system. This time Davey and the rest of the band could hear Bear's voice in the overhead sound system as he spoke into the black rectangle. Bear explained that he had improved the communications system to allow the band to reach him wherever he was.

"It will be like having you with us on our journey," said Rubin. "Totally cool!"

"This is all incredibly impressive, Bear. Wow, thank you. I don't understand how any of this works, but I'm glad that it does," Davey said. "I do have one question. What about the blue button on the dashboard? That one caught my eye when I walked in because it's blue like my crushed velvet seat. Why doesn't it have a label?"

"Yeah, just ignore that one. Ignore it. I'm still perfecting the technology. It's better if you don't press it. In fact, I wouldn't press it. I can add a 'DO NOT USE' label if you'd like," said Bear.

"A label would be good if it's about safety," Davey replied, thinking about how he still didn't know what the blue button did, but that he wouldn't press it.

The band used the rest of the afternoon to load the bus in preparation for their road trip. Maggie had created a checklist of everything they needed to bring. She checked off items as they loaded them. They put the sound system, amps, speakers, cables, drums, keyboard, supplies, canned goods, and water in the under-bus storage. They put the guitars on the couches so they could play at a moment's notice. They each put their personal items and clothes in their bunk storage areas. They made sure the kitchen had all the utensils and cookware they needed. They filled a cabinet with snacks, like space-saving tubes of Pringle's Newfangled Potato Chips, all four varieties of Pop-Tarts, and easy-to-use drink mixes, like Tang and both chocolate and strawberry Nestle's Quik.

After Maggie confirmed that everything on her checklist was on the bus, they retired to the house for an evening of relaxation. Bear stayed for dinner and then went home.

The next morning, Davey woke up early to get the coffee started and put a kettle on the stove for tea. It had become routine to meet in the kitchen for breakfast on the weekends, and the band decided they would have a Sunday-sized breakfast before heading out on the road. By the time everyone came down to the kitchen, the aroma of coffee was strong. Davey made bacon and eggs. Joey cooked omelets by request.

Maggie said, "I have a checklist of the perishables we need to put in the bus's refrigerator. We can pull the bus up to the house and load it on our way out."

"Great," said Davey. "I know we bought extra milk and cheese."

"And we have Tupperware containers full of diced fruit and vegetables," Stella added. "We'll be on the road for over nine weeks. We can refill those periodically throughout our trip."

"I'm amped for this adventure," Joey said. "We'll be playing at six festivals. That's six chances to create something new!"

"Yeah man, we'll have six unique and mind-blowing experiences with the audience," agreed Rubin. "Hopefully all recorded."

Davey added, "And we'll be visiting fun places and learning cool things along the way."

Everyone agreed that this would be an extraordinary summer! After they finished eating, they cleaned up the kitchen and Davey brought the bus up to the house, being sure to put on the parking brake. With her checklist, Maggie led the effort to load the perishable items. Within an hour, the band had everything they needed on the bus and they were ready to roll. As the others sat down on the u-shaped couches, Davey said that he'd be right back.

He went inside the house one last time to make sure it was ready to be closed up for so many weeks. He was glad that Bear would come by to tend to the garden and keep an eye on things. He trusted Bear. There was just something about him that Davey liked. They had met when Davey's wife was ill, and Bear had been a good companion. It's almost like Bear had picked the perfect time to arrive.

Davey checked the windows and looked out the front door. He saw antelope in the yard and stepped onto the front porch to watch them graze. He stood there silently, thinking for a few moments about how his wife would have enjoyed this day. He also thought that with his new friends and their music, the house was no longer silent, and he was no longer lonely. He realized that the music had never stopped.

He closed the front door and walked towards the back of the house. Davey smiled as he neared the bus. He could hear laughter, strumming guitars, and the voices of his friends. Climbing into his crushed blue velvet driver's seat, Davey turned to look at the others and said, "Devils Tower, here we come!"

He sat down, released the parking brake, and rolled the bus forward. "So many roads to ride," he said quietly to himself.

EPILOGUE

"Franklin's Tower"
— Grateful Dead

Stanley walked through the alumni center to the 1960s exhibit. This afternoon was the first evidence of significant change in the artifacts on display. The picture of The Bed Heads now included Cherise, their touring bus. He exhaled with relief, now aware that he'd been holding his breath. His time bridge was still intact and working. Rather than reveal the past all at once, the connection was parallel, updating bit by bit. He was glad he'd asked the Sinclair station in Kaycee to stock extra fuel filters. The horse hotel next to it was cool and he wondered if it was still there.

He quickly turned on his tablet and searched for "The Bed Heads." The results included a few more articles and two concert videos from a tour. He smiled with satisfaction; the band's history was beginning to change.

He prepared himself to go back. Although they didn't know it, The Bed Heads were going to need him at Devils Tower. But first, he wanted to try something new. He'd heard that Frontier Brewery was now serving coffee. If The Bed Heads had taught him anything, it was to take coffee seriously. And he wanted to ask the folks at Frontier about their upcoming trivia nights. He hoped that Geeks Who Drink Pub Quizzes had a groovy 1960s edition. At this point, he could probably win on his own without the help of a team. Especially if the questions were about festivals, music, or retro technology. Maybe foods. There was still something special about Jell-O.

It was time to get that hot coffee. While leaving the alumni center, he glanced back at the display. He chuckled as one other new addition caught his eye. A container of Tang.

Stay tuned for more adventures with The Bed Heads!

wriwksp.com/backstagepass

#TheBedHeadsWYO

ABOUT THE AUTHOR

Cody Ashbury is the magic that happens when writers join forces to create groovy adventures, just for you. It's when worlds collide and the sultry city of San Francisco meets the open frontier of Wyoming. In the nut world, it's the joy of finding sweet and spicy pecans.

We want you to love our characters as much as we do. To keep the kozmic exchange of good vibes and positive energy going, we've curated far out playlists, designed some boss merchandise, and collected some stellar pictures, videos, and links. Swing by our pad at https://wriwksp.com/backstagepass and see what you can find. We hope you dig it.